El Dorado County Library

Donated by
Kate Parkhurst

THE INVASION OF THE CAVITY CREATURES

By Kate Parkhurst

Illustrated by Eloy Claudio

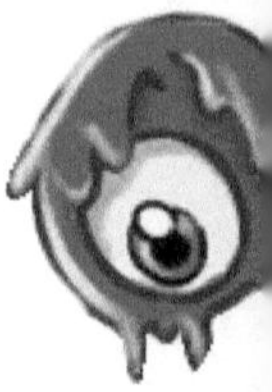

To contact either one, please visit *www.kateparkhurst.com*

To the class that inspired the
Toothpaste Avenger from the start.
Keep it up Busy Bees!
To my wonderful husband—thank you!

— K.P.

To mom for forcing me to brush my teeth.
To Mandee for reminding me to keep
visiting the people of Tongue Town.

— E.C.

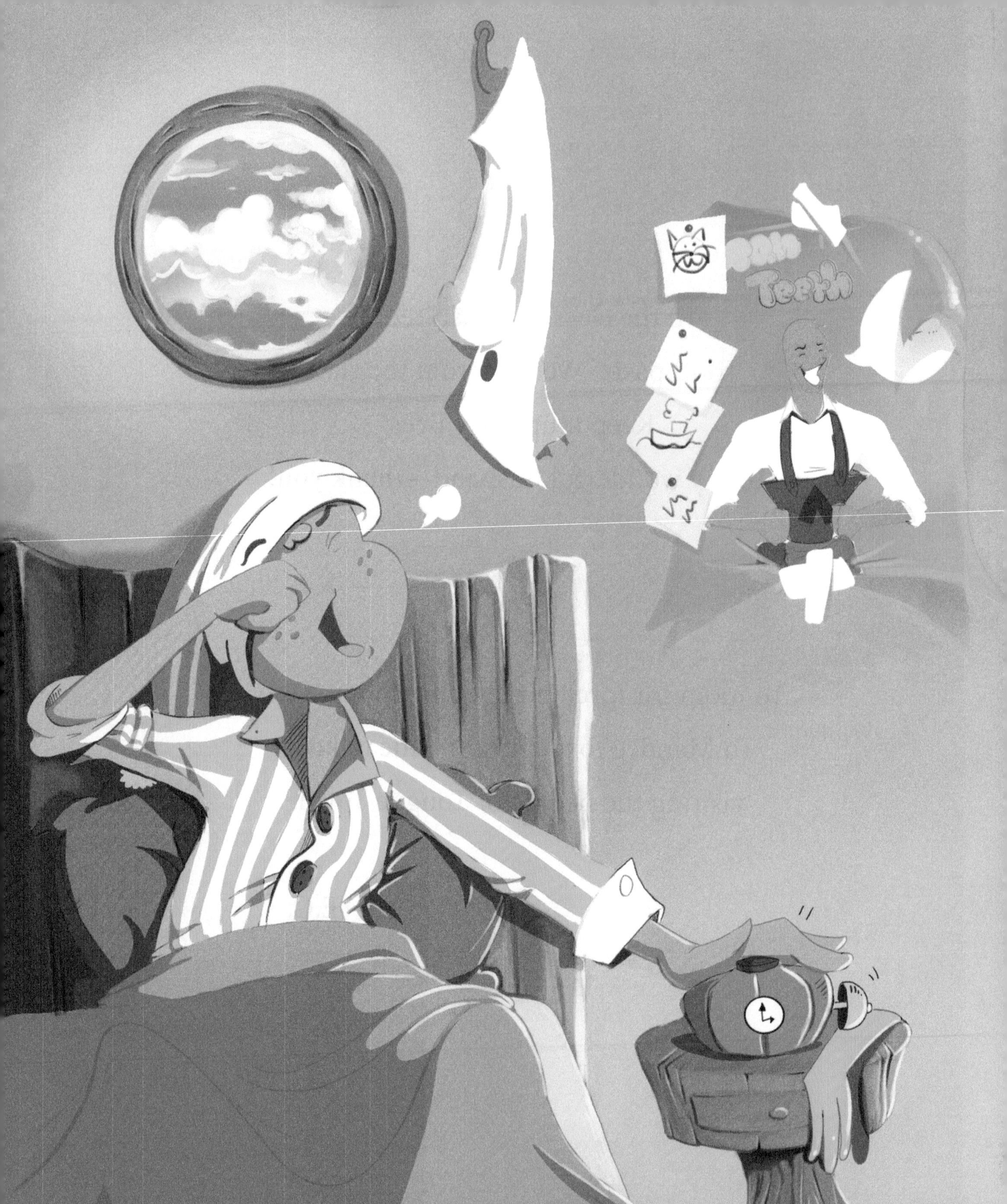
Teeth

Bobby Brusher lazily rubbed his eyes and slowly turned off his alarm clock. "Ugh," he moaned.

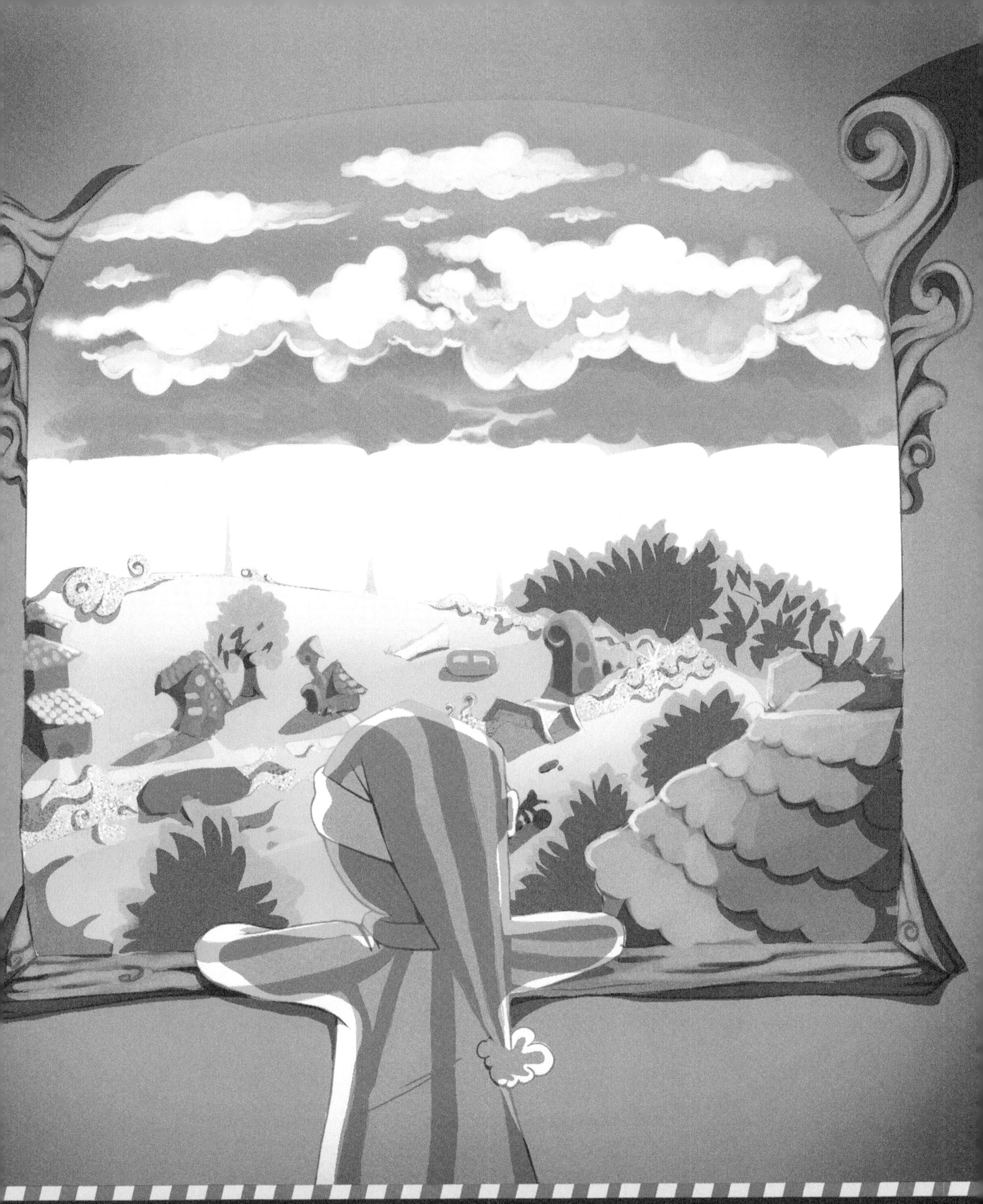

He glanced out of his window at Tongue Town. The sun was glistening off of the white Molar Mountains, Bubble Gum Toothpaste River was flowing lazily through town, and Root Canal was crowded with workers getting on and off the barges for the day's work.

"It's way too nice to go to work today," Bobby decided.

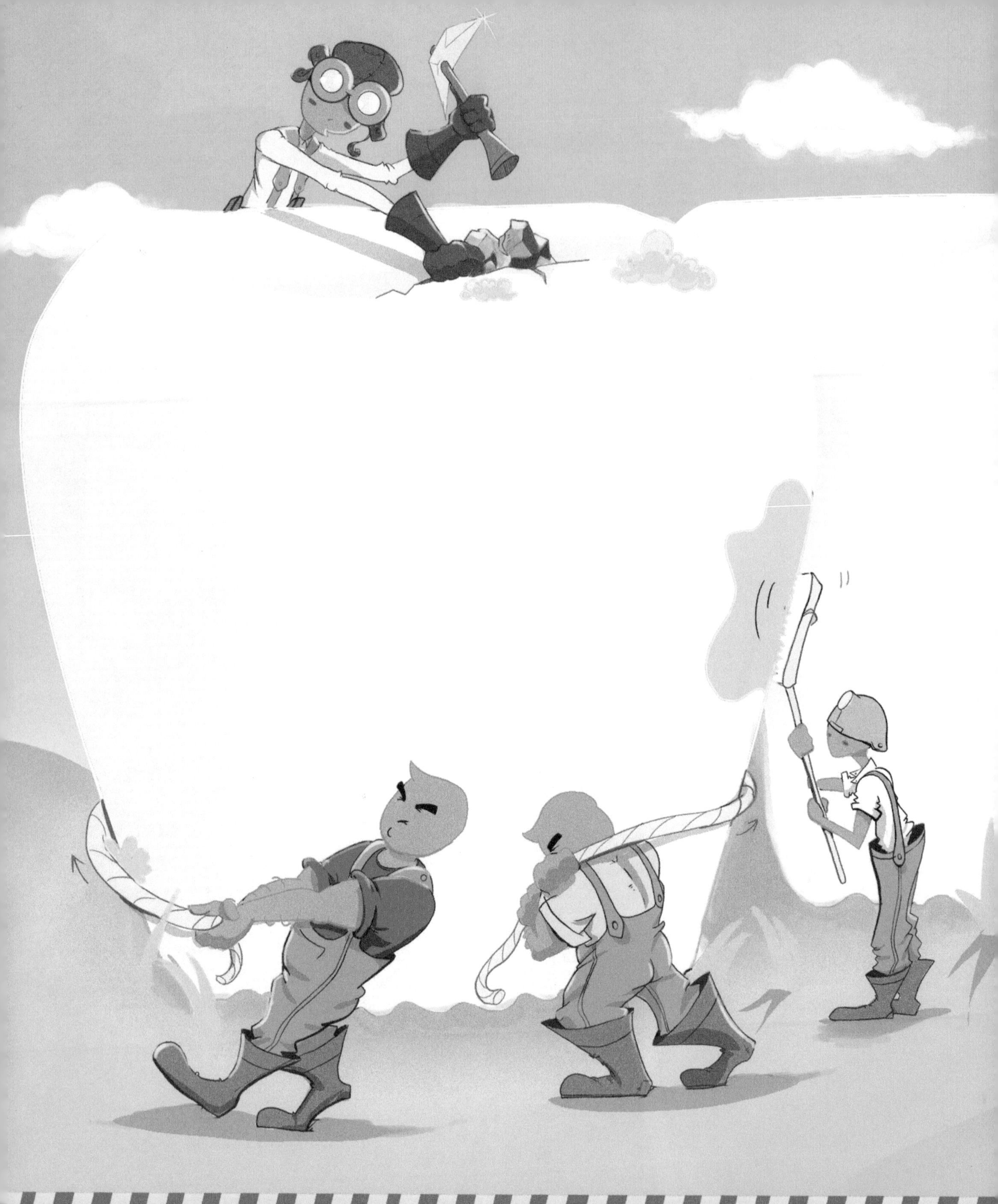

Like everyday in Tongue Town, today each person was busy with a very important job. Brushers brushed in wide, round circles. Pickers pulled plaque from hard-to-reach places. Flossers polished tiny crevices using a special kind of string.

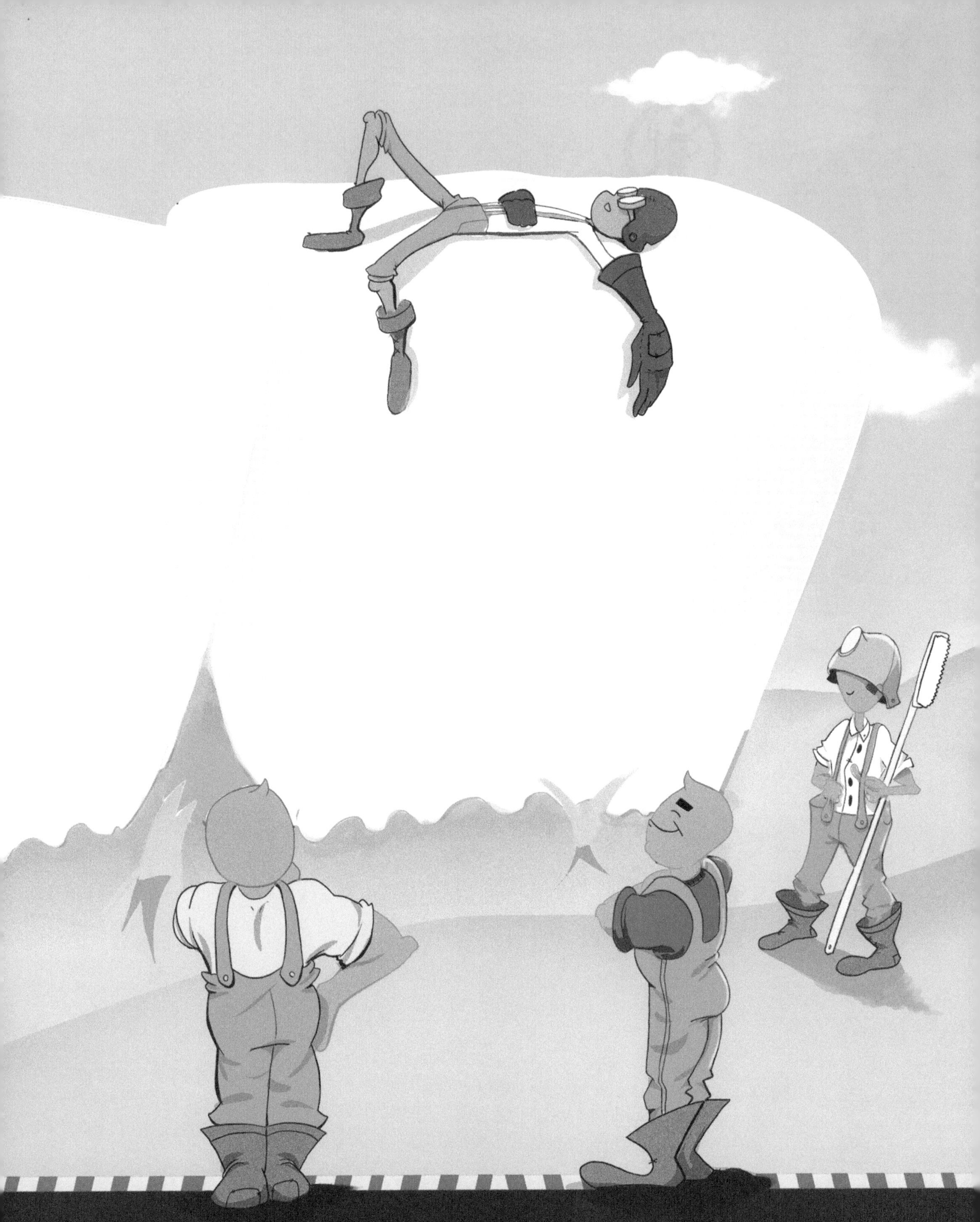

The tiny people of Tongue Town were proud of all the dutiful work they did keeping the Molar Mountains white, shiny, and clean. They knew that it kept the green, slimy Cavity Creatures from taking over.

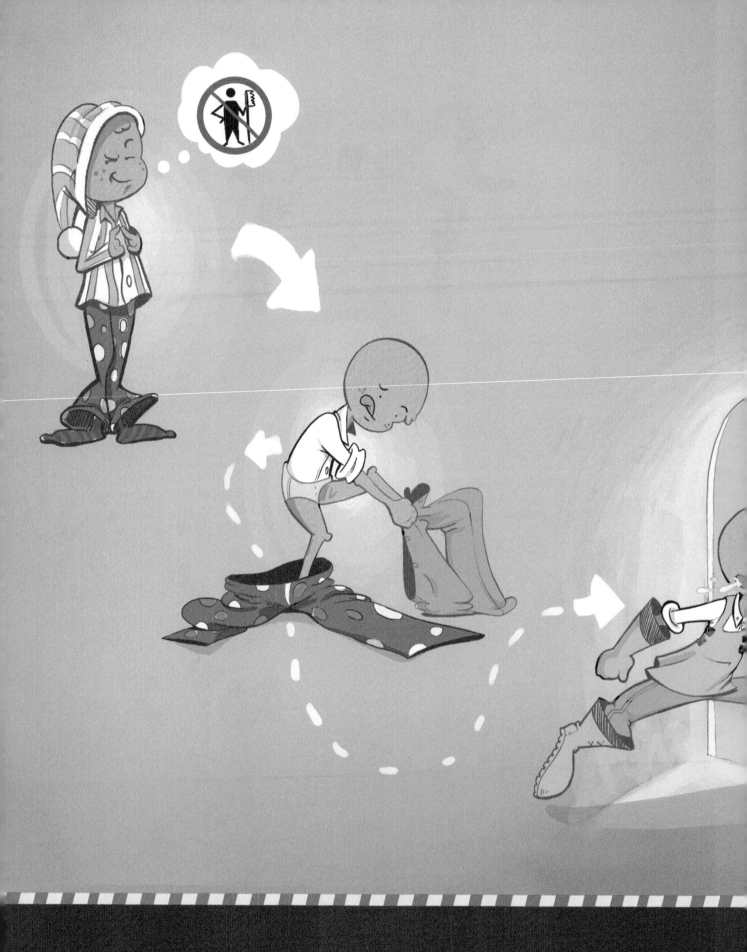

Today, Bobby Brusher decided that since all the other brushers were hard at work, he would take the day off.   He ran from his house and jumped into the Bubble Gum Toothpaste River with a *SPLASH*!

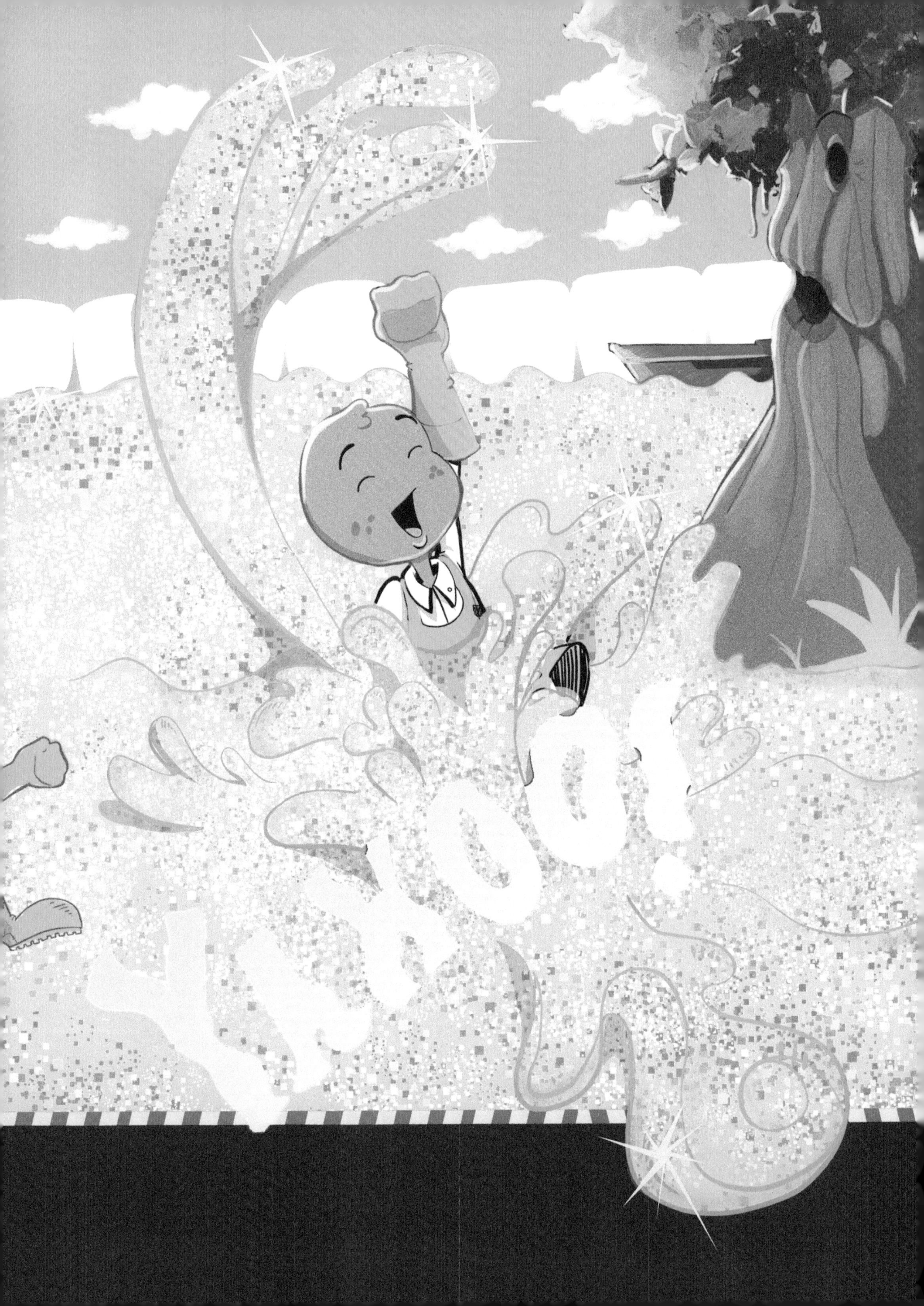
YAHOO!

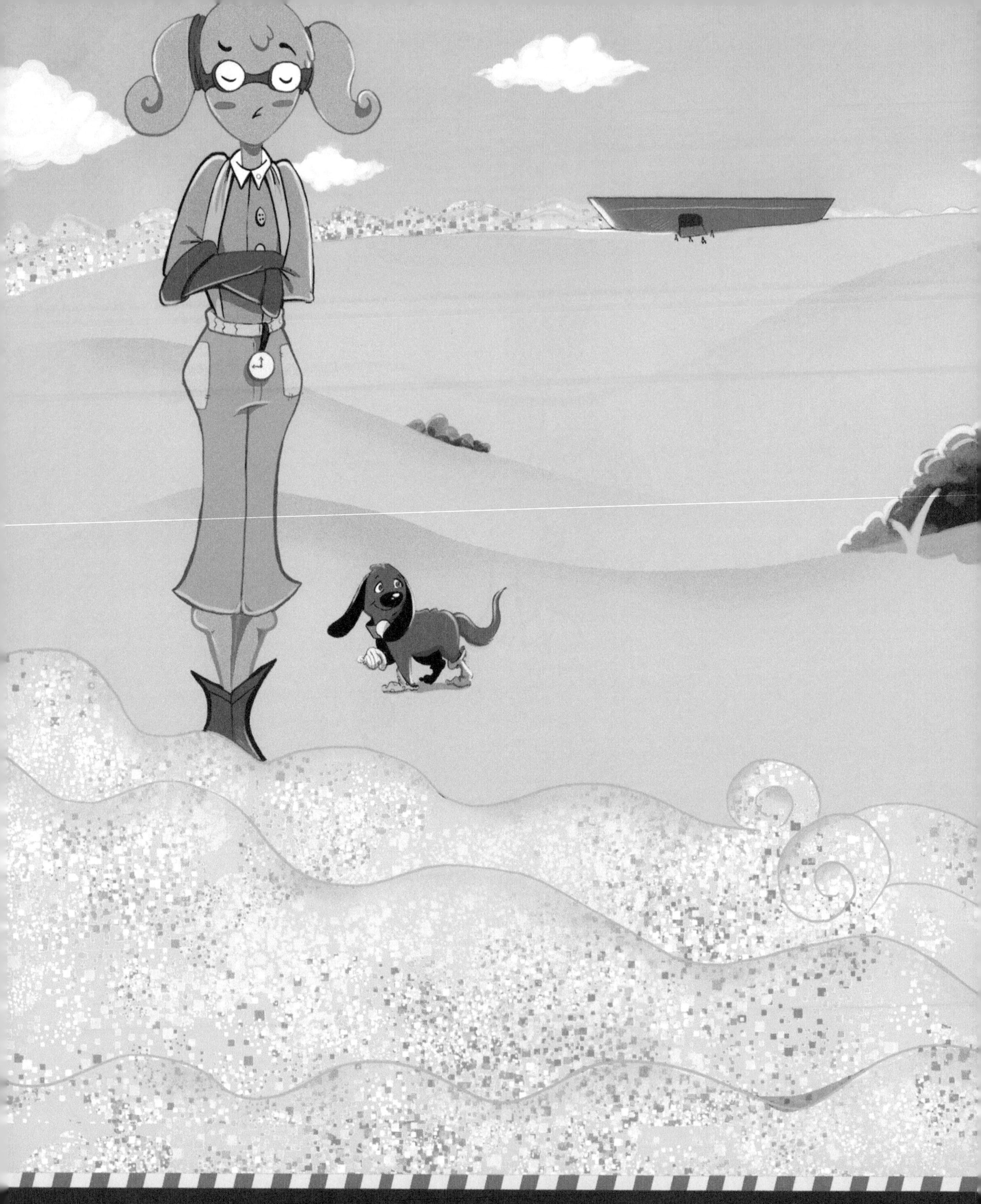

As Bobby was swimming, his best friend, Penelope Picker, was walking by on her way to work.

“Bobby! What are you doing? You are supposed to be brushing,” she said.

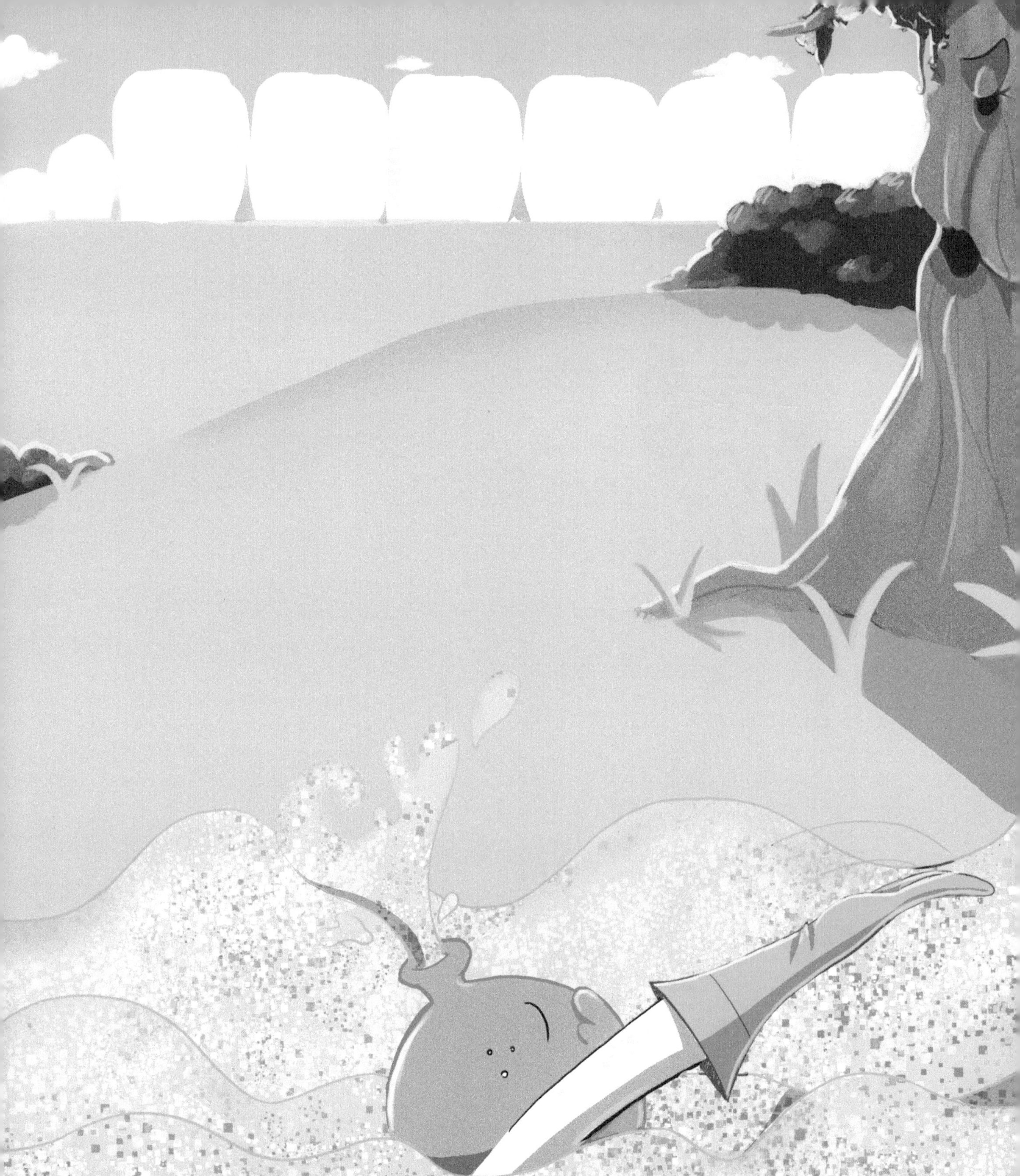

‘Hey Penelope! Come in! The river is so nice, the day is bright, and it’s not like anyone will notice we aren’t working,” replied Bobby.

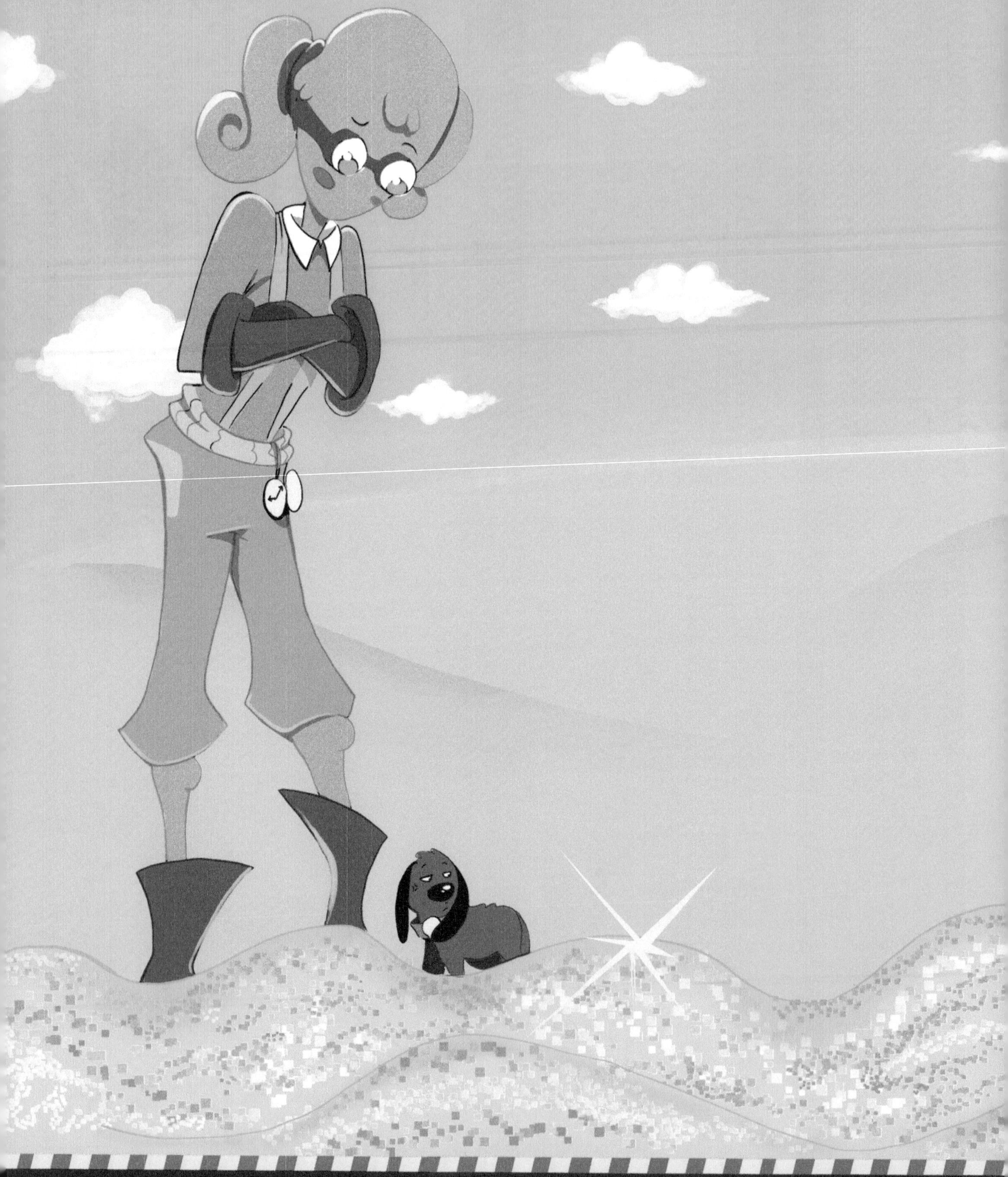

"Bobby, you know we aren't supposed to take time off! The Cavity Creatures could invade at any moment. Everything we do to keep the Molar Mountains clean could be ruined," explained Penelope.

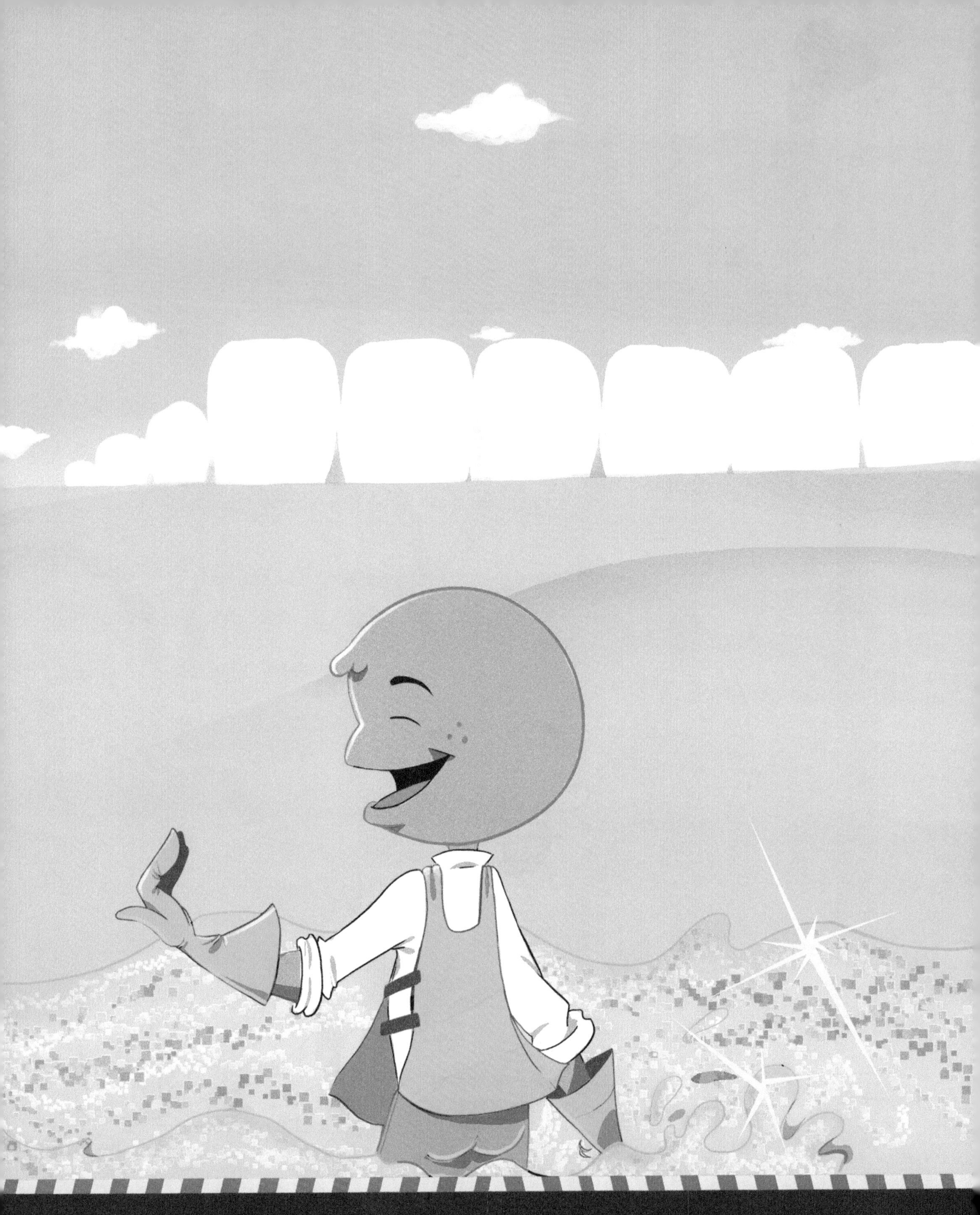

"Awe, Penelope, come on! It's just one day. You should feel how warm the river is. It tingles too! You'd love it. Besides, Peter, Pepper, and Papa are all picking. Billy, Bruno, Babs, and Bubba are all brushing. And you know the Flossers – they'll floss till they drop. There's nothing to worry about," Bobby said.

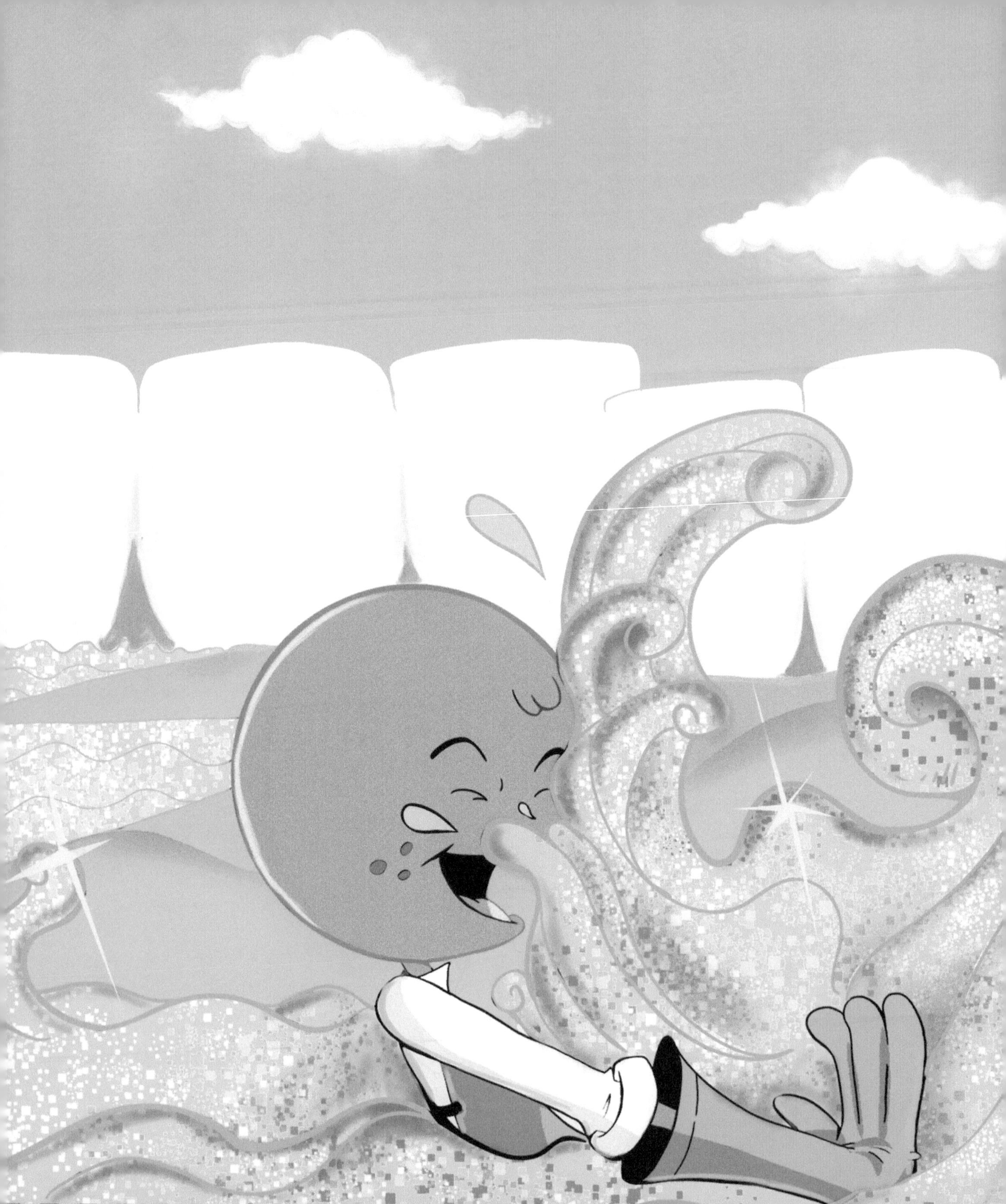

I really don't think it's a good idea," Penelope said as she timidly stepped into the river. "Wow! This feels great!"

Before long...

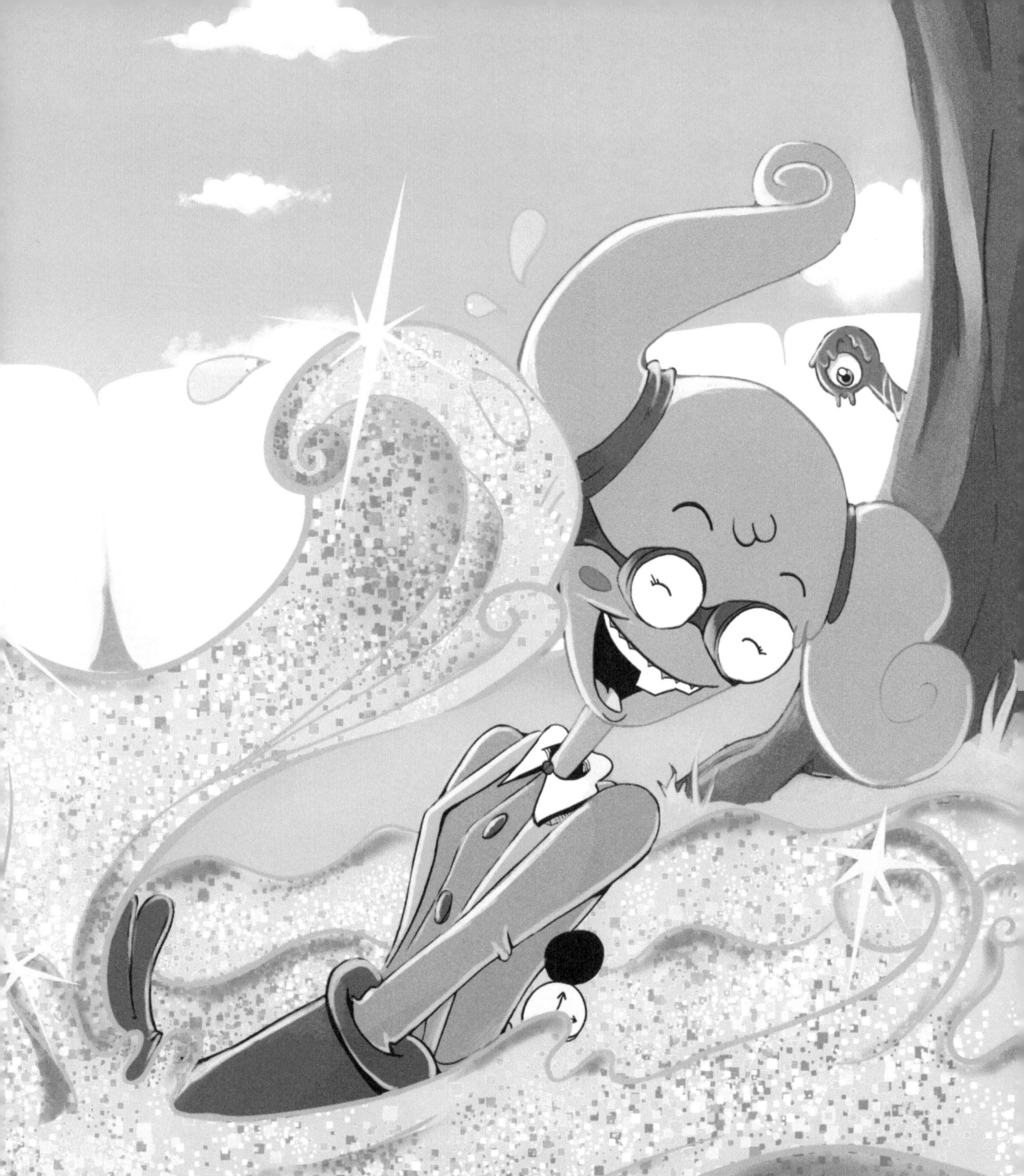

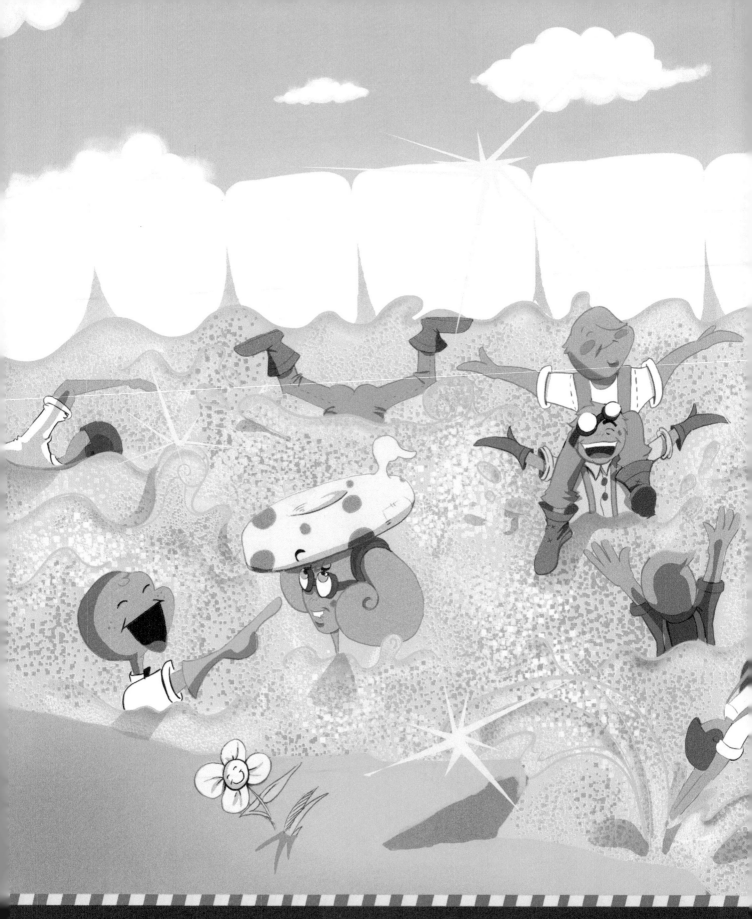

"Hey, Fran Flosser, come join us!" Bobby yelled as she walked by on her way to work. "Tie some of your string up in the tree, too!"

Other Brushers on their way to work noticed the fun these three were having and decided to join them.

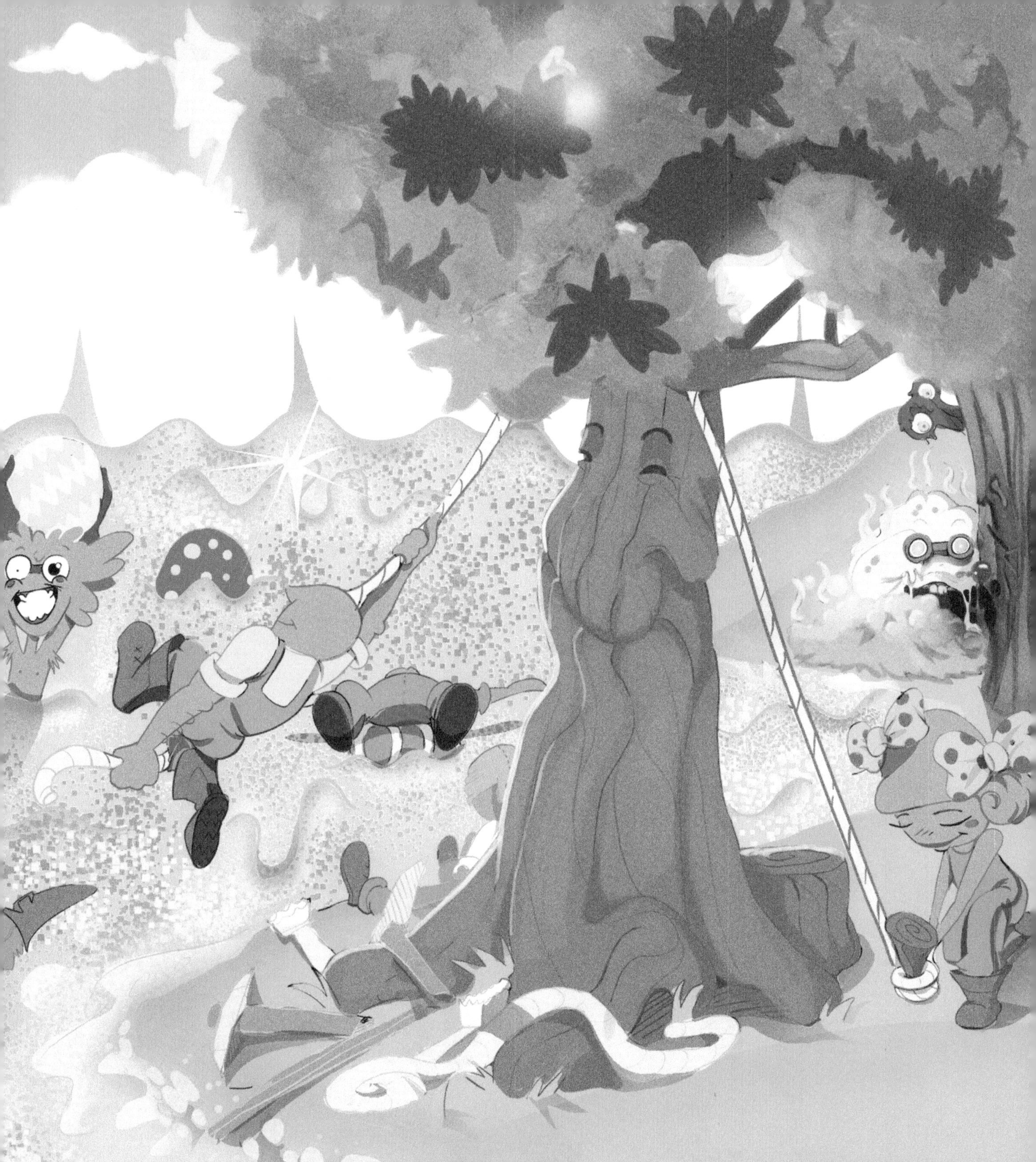

When the Pickers saw what the Brushers were doing, they dropped their tools and jumped right into the Bubble Gum Toothpaste River.

Soon, even the Flossers were swinging from trees into the river with a splash!

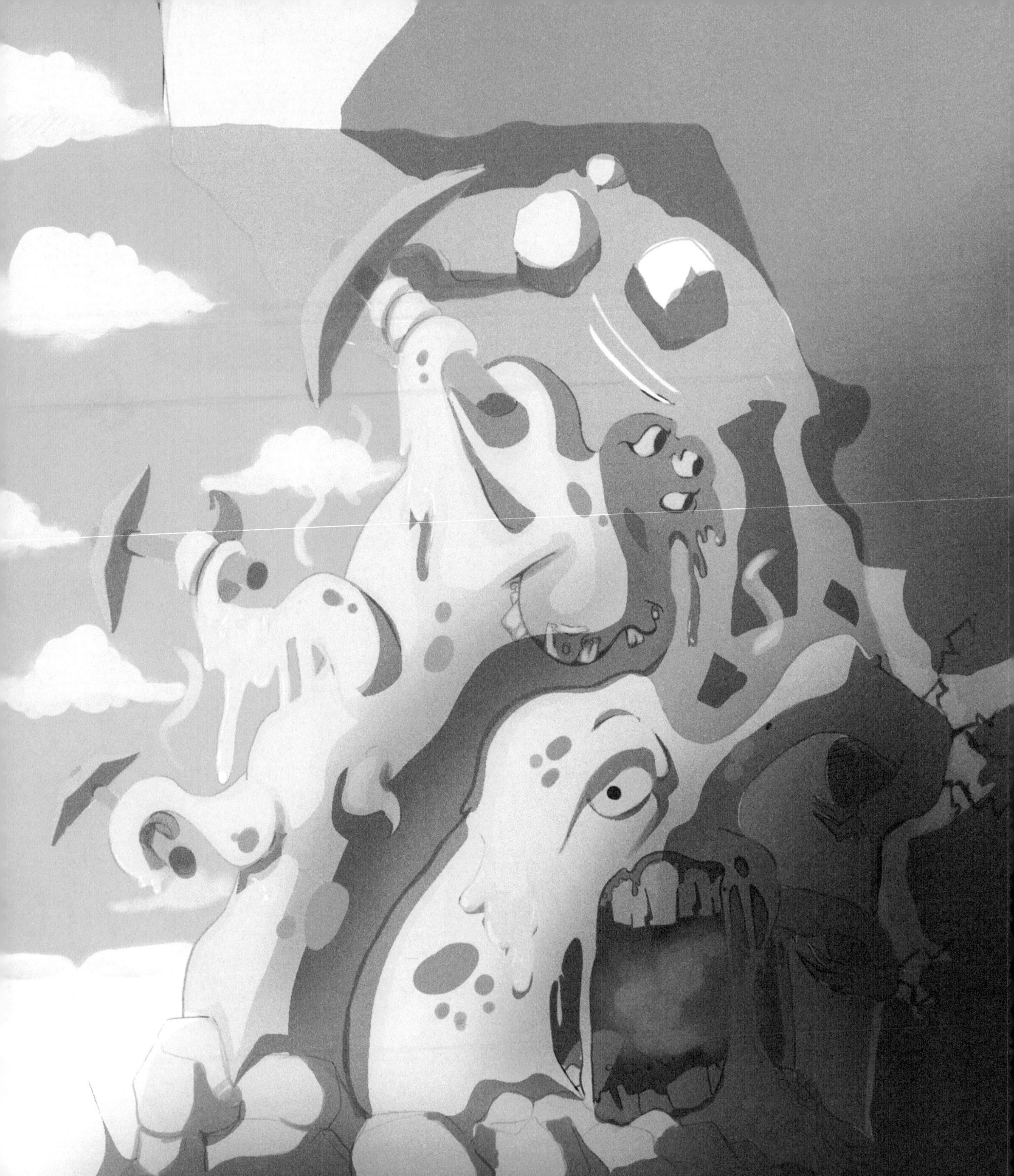

While the Brushers, Pickers, and Flossers laughed and played in the river, two Cavity Creatures seized the moment. The icky blobs crept up the largest mountain, Incisor Incline, and began digging furiously to make themselves a deep, dark, moldy cave.

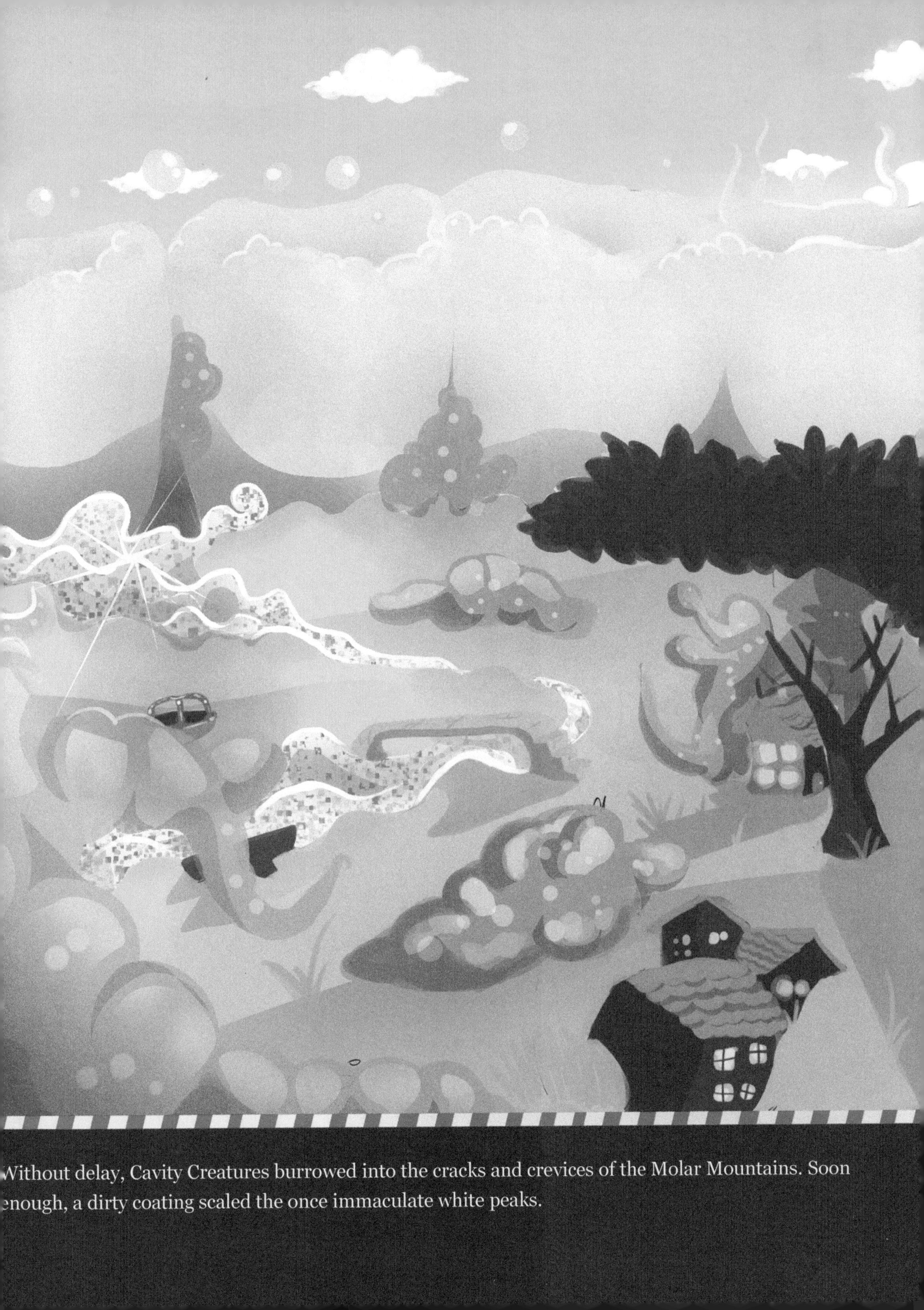

Vithout delay, Cavity Creatures burrowed into the cracks and crevices of the Molar Mountains. Soon
enough, a dirty coating scaled the once immaculate white peaks.

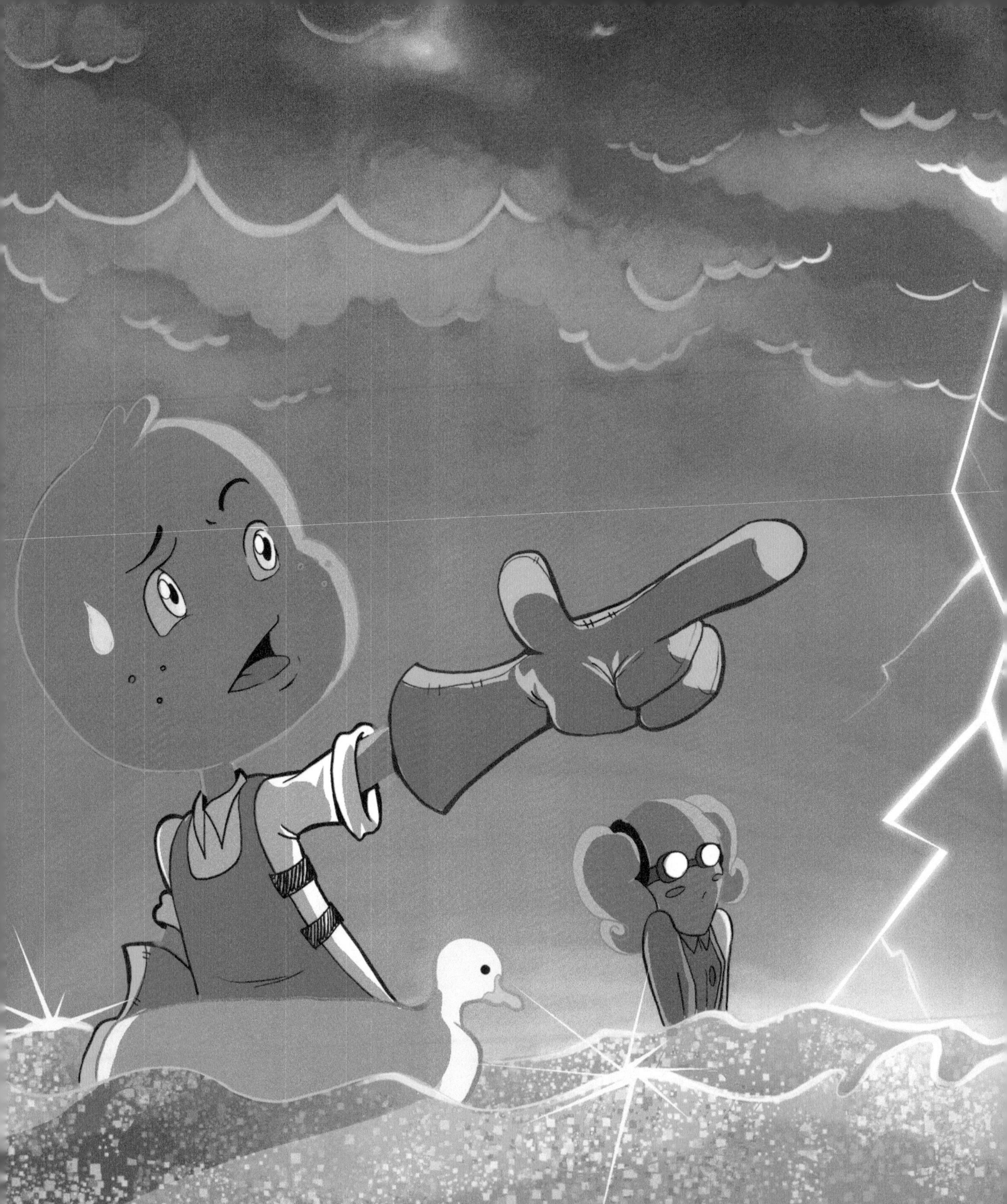

Bobby was floating on his back in the river when he noticed that the Molar Mountains didn't look right. "Look!" he piped up. "Is that a plague of plaque?"

"It is!" yelped Penelope Picker. "Oh, no! What do we do?"

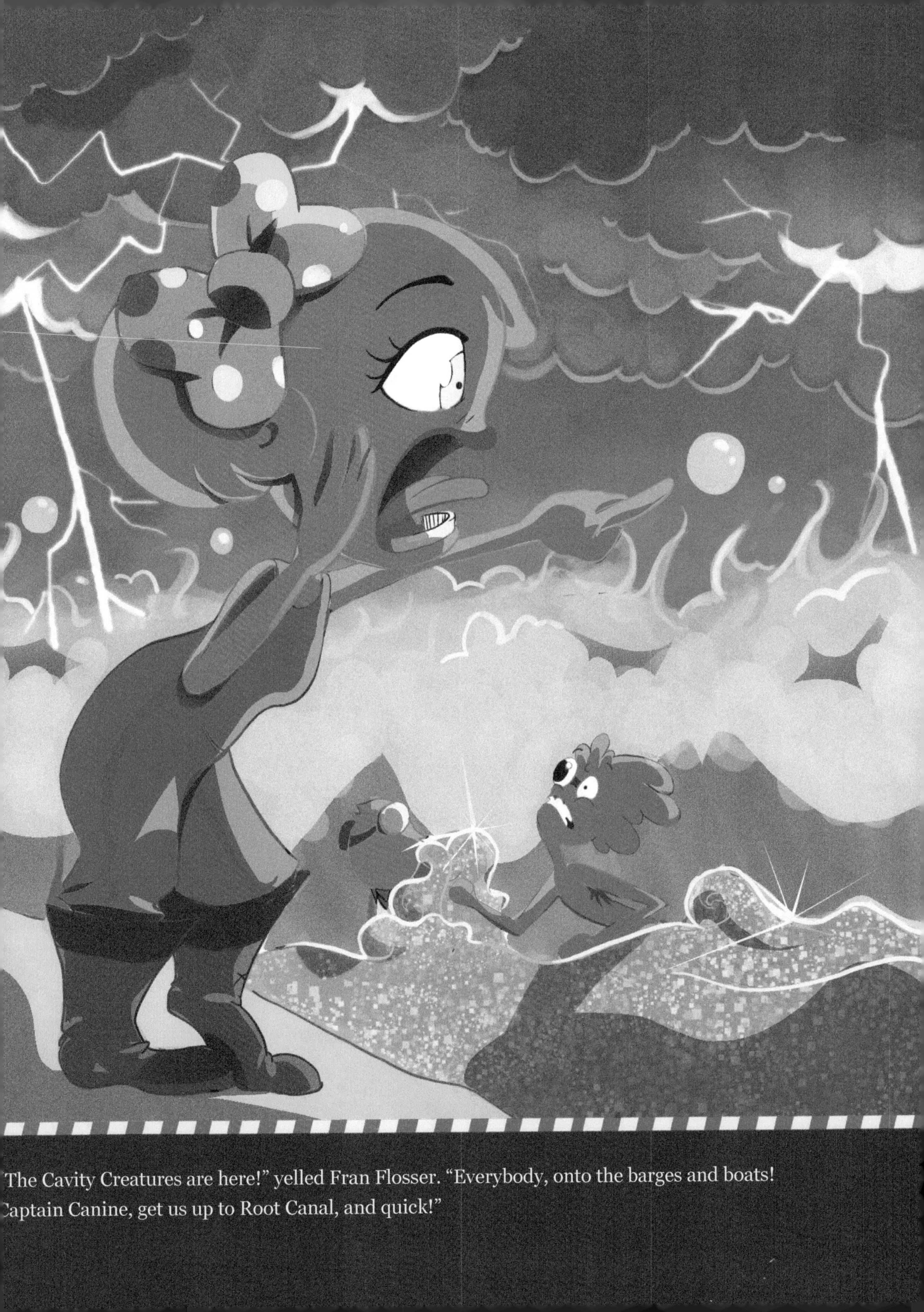

"The Cavity Creatures are here!" yelled Fran Flosser. "Everybody, onto the barges and boats! Captain Canine, get us up to Root Canal, and quick!"

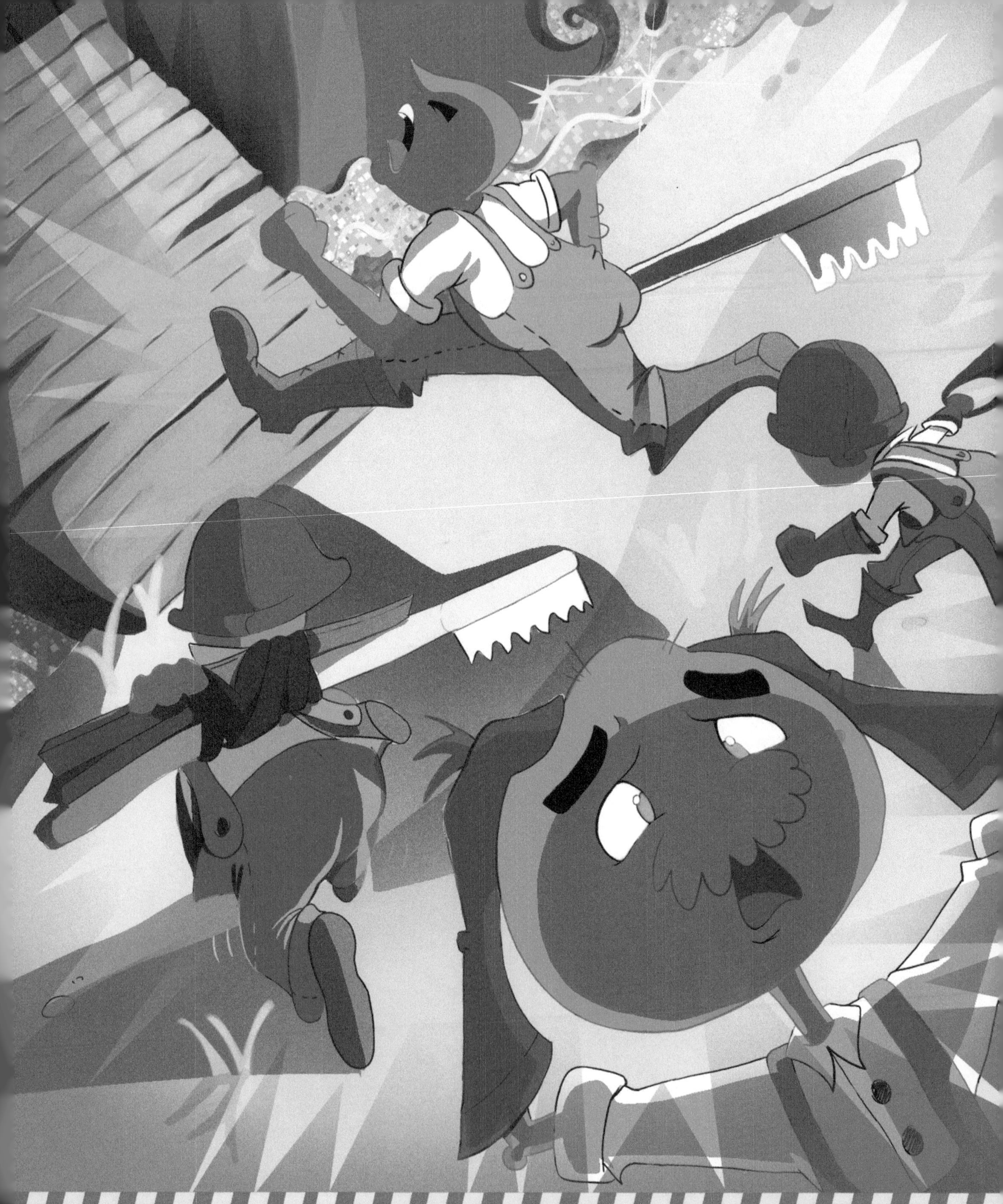

Everyone started to panic. They ran from the river, grabbed their tools, and jumped onto the barges.

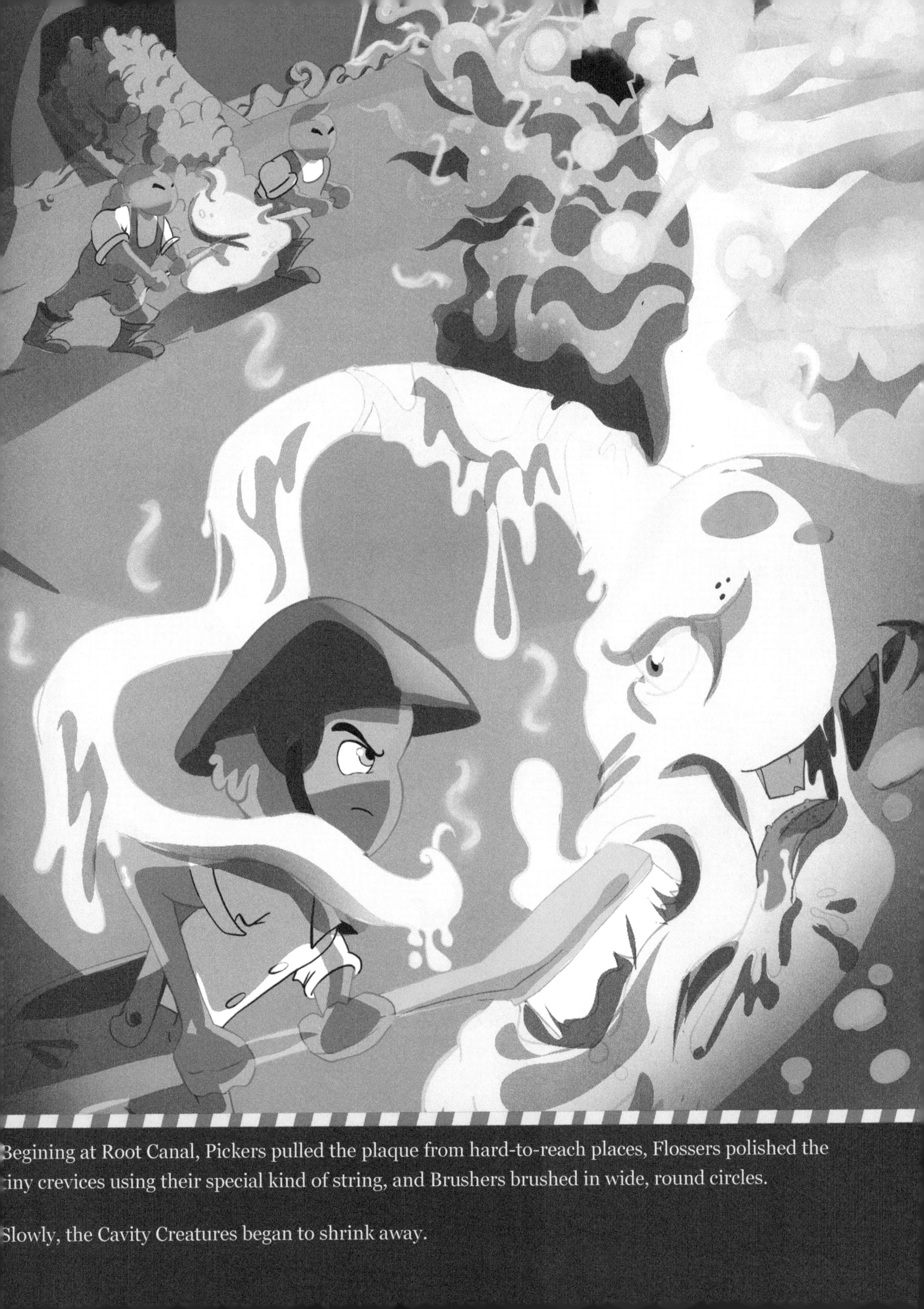

Begining at Root Canal, Pickers pulled the plaque from hard-to-reach places, Flossers polished the tiny crevices using their special kind of string, and Brushers brushed in wide, round circles.

Slowly, the Cavity Creatures began to shrink away.

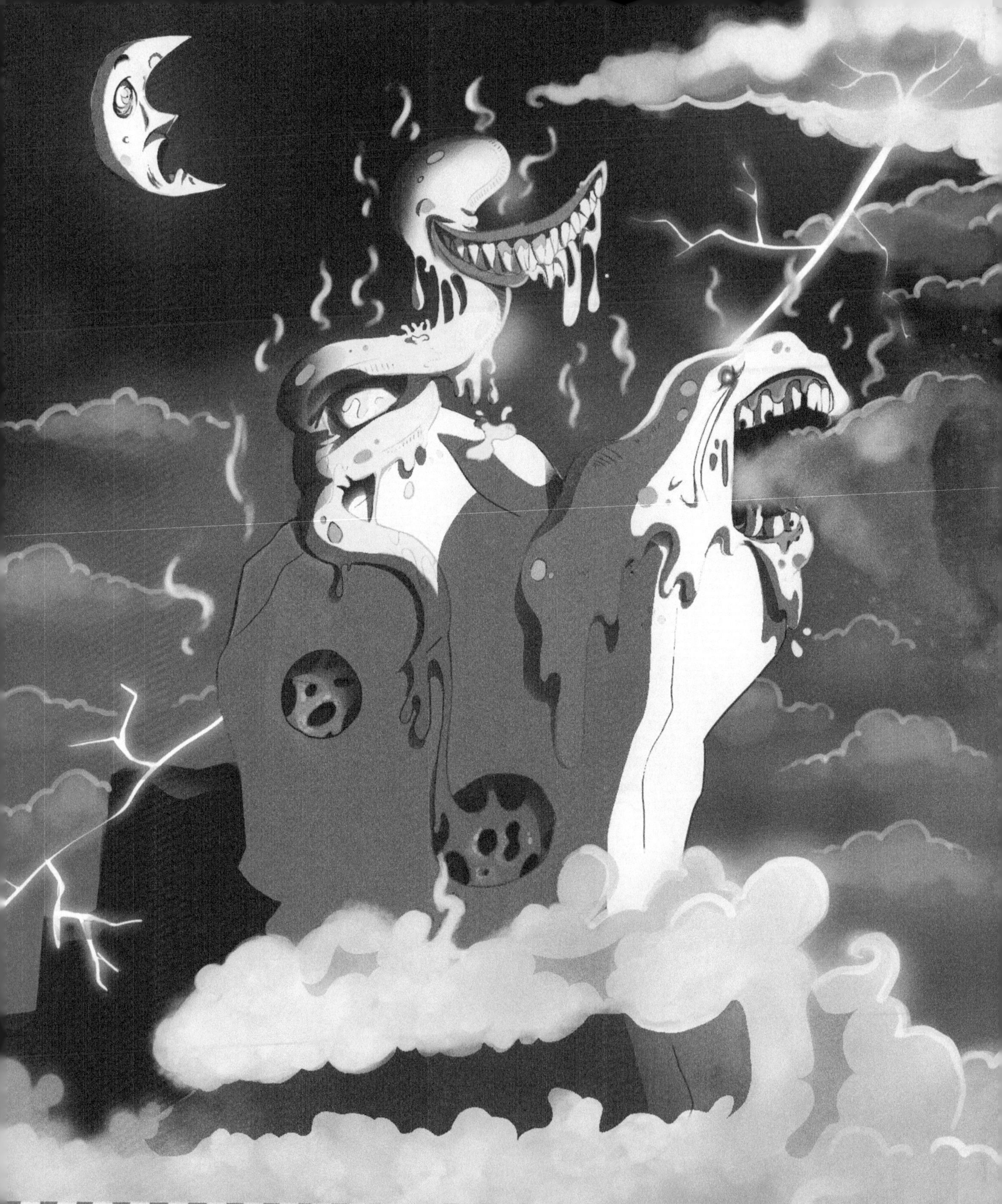

Yet, one problem remained. Incisor Incline was the most difficult to reach of all the Molar Mountains, and it appeared as though the Cavity Creatures had dug in deep and were not going to leave.

Frustrated, the Brushers, Pickers, and Flossers held a special town meeting in front of the Bubble Gum Toothpaste River.

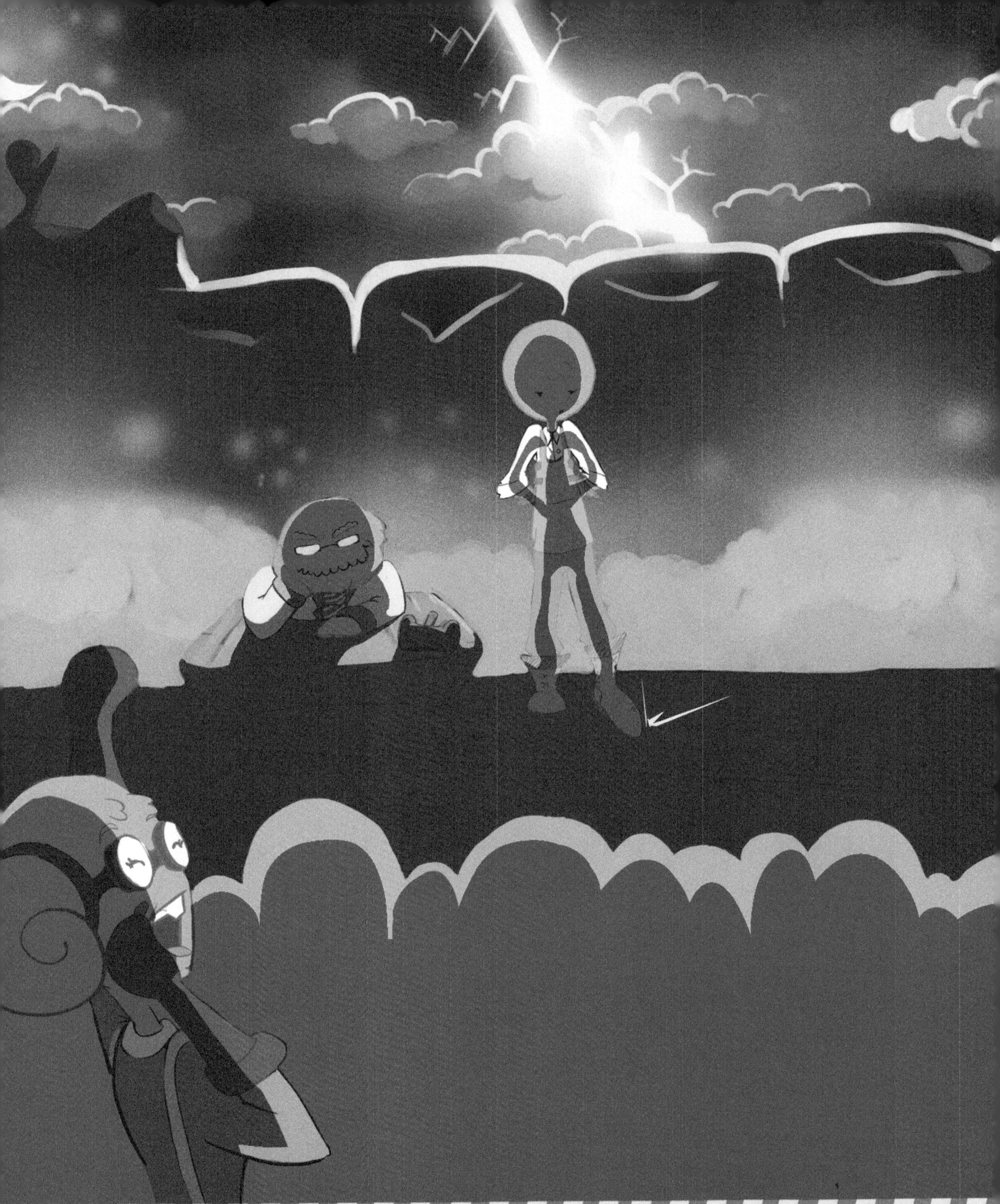

Holding his hands behind his back, Bobby sheepishly dug his toe in the ground and quietly suggested, "Why don't we call the Toothpaste Avenger?"

"He has a belt full of tools that can help us," assured Penelope Picker.

Everyone agreed this was a job for the ever-trusted Toothpaste Avenger.

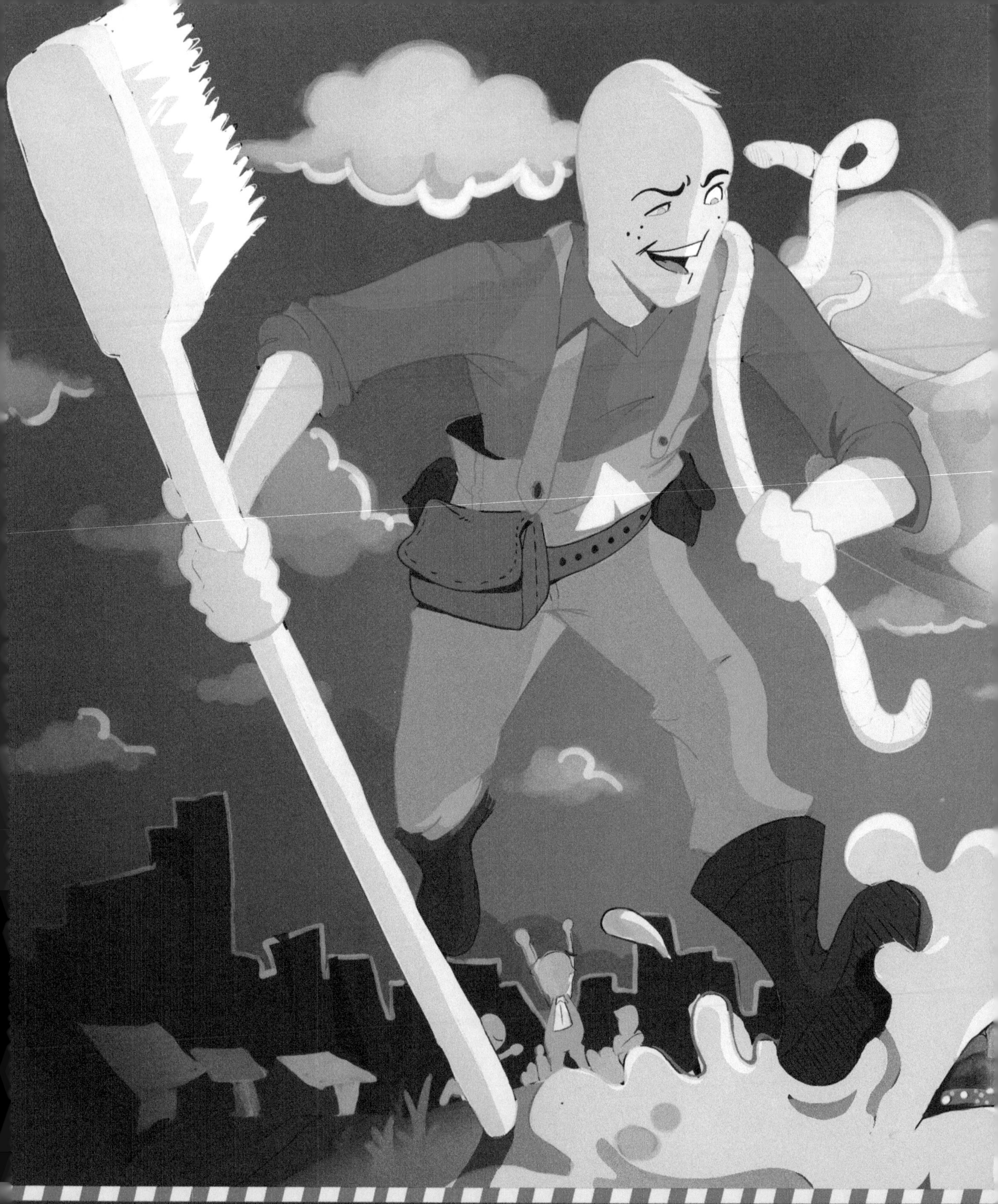

With his tools strapped around his waist, the Toothpaste Avenger rushed into town ready for battle. Scared by the enormity of his brush and the sharpness of his pick, the creatures shrank back into their deep, dark, moldy cave. The Toothpaste Avenger set to work brushing and polishing.

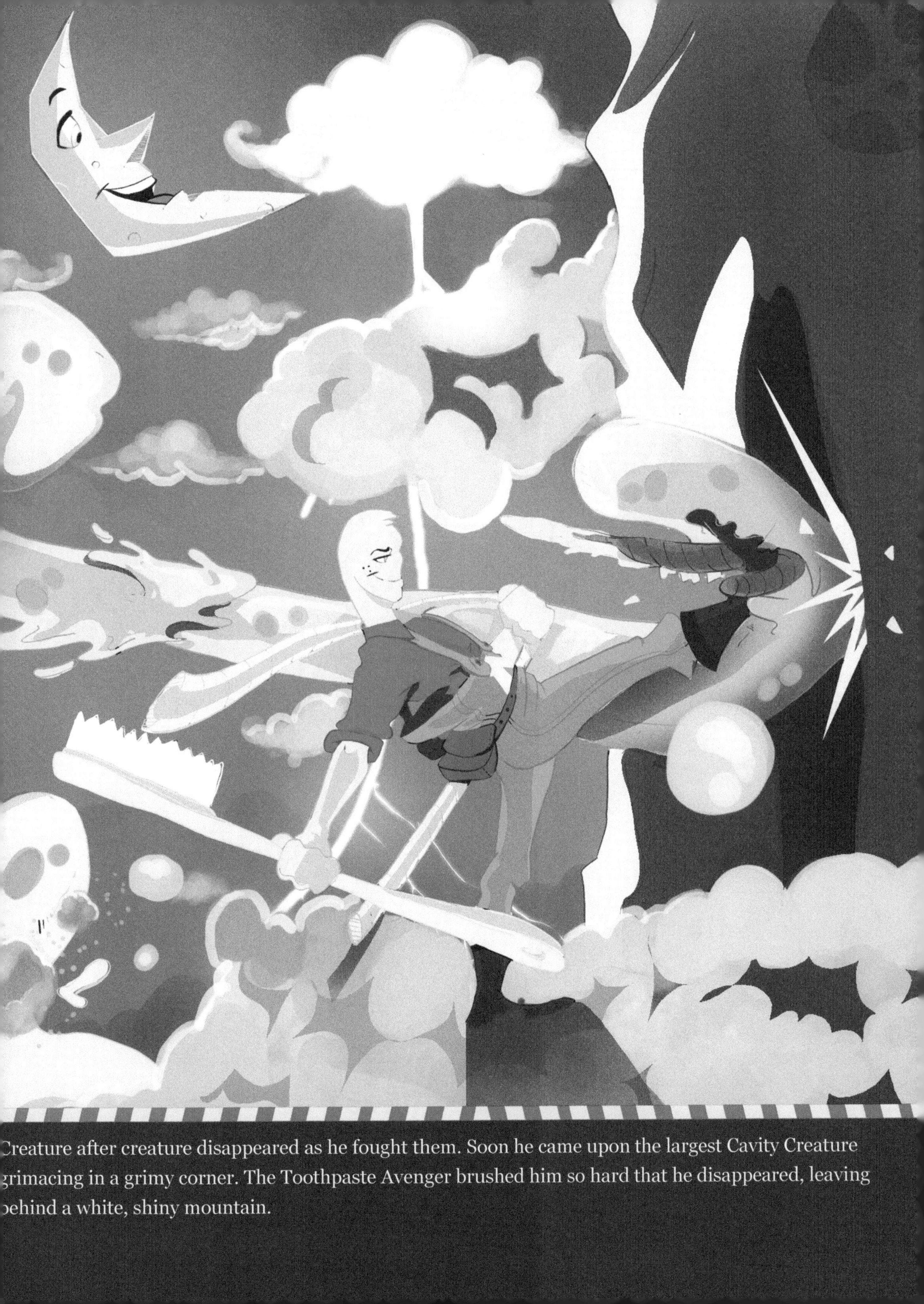

Creature after creature disappeared as he fought them. Soon he came upon the largest Cavity Creature grimacing in a grimy corner. The Toothpaste Avenger brushed him so hard that he disappeared, leaving behind a white, shiny mountain.

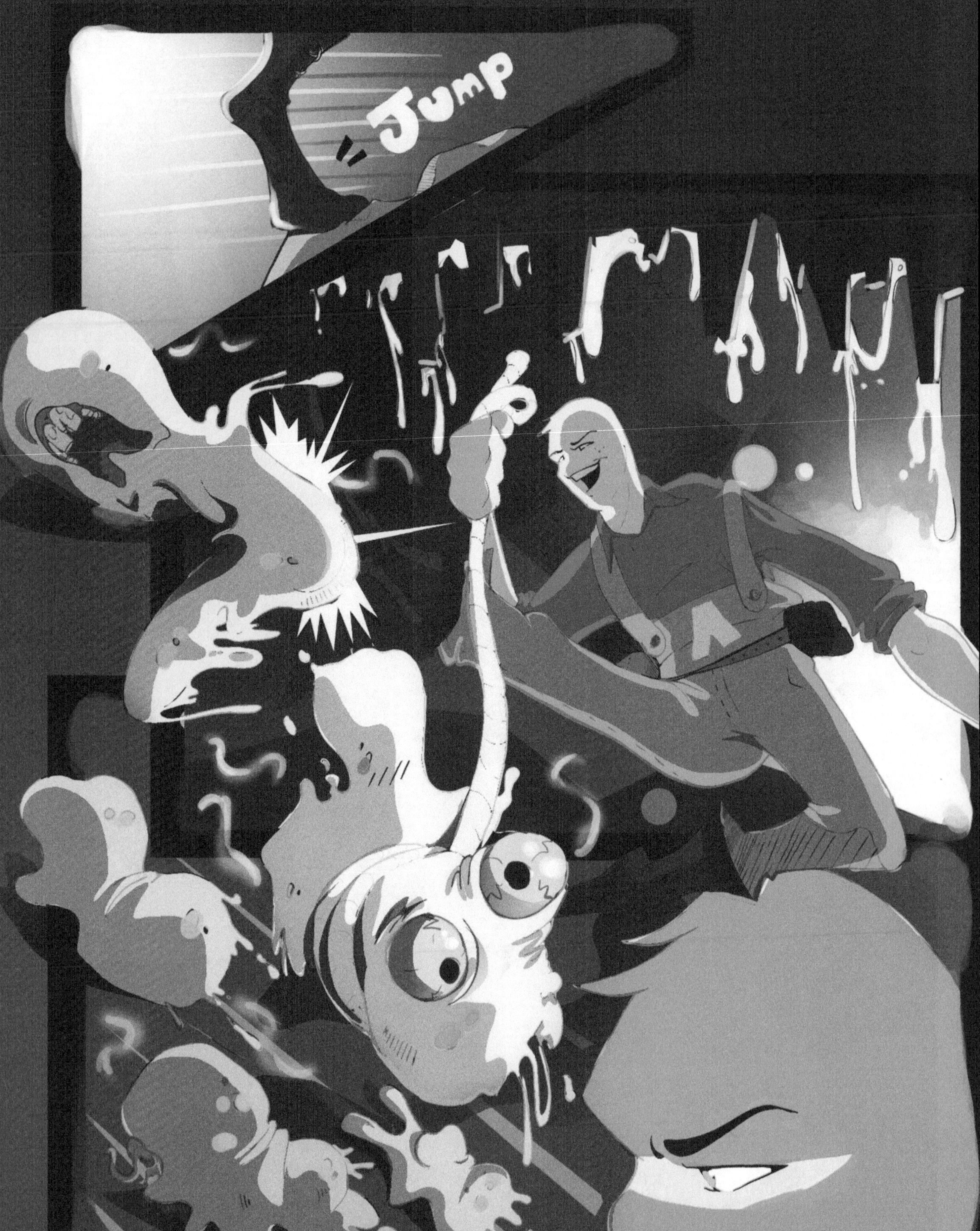
Jump

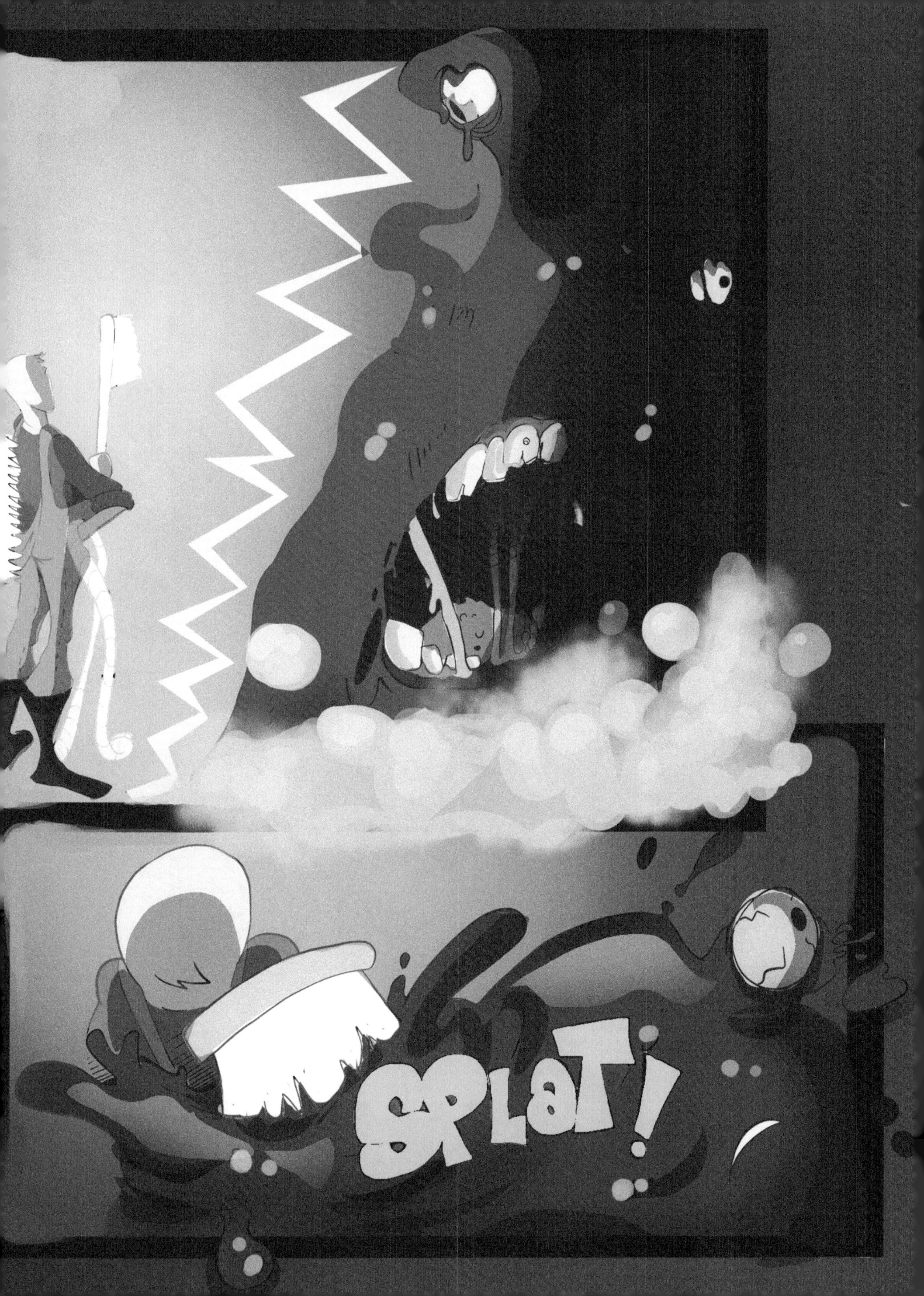
SPLAT!

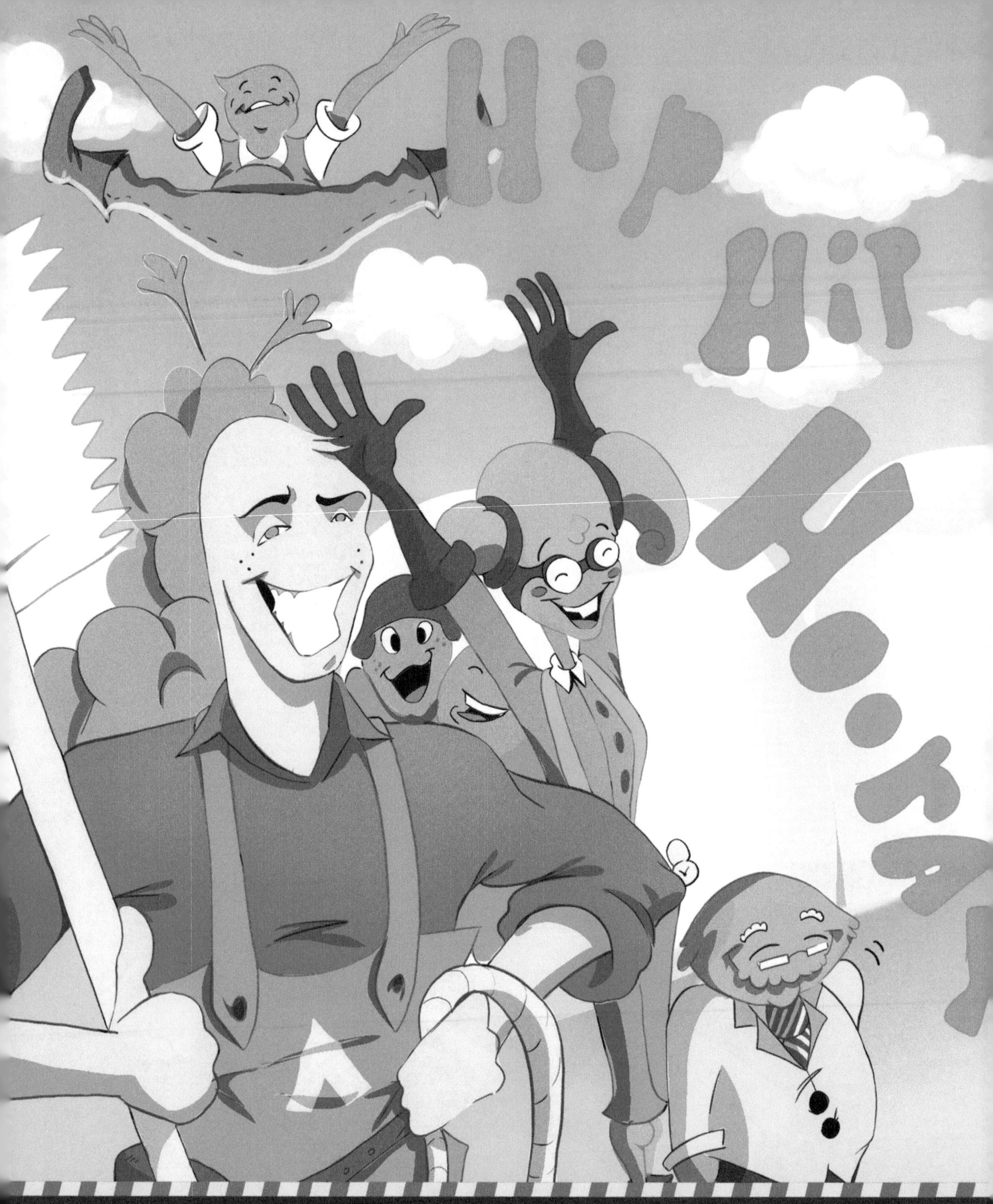
Hip
Hip
Hoora

When the Toothpaste Avenger emerged from his work, tools in hand, the people of Tongue Town cheered

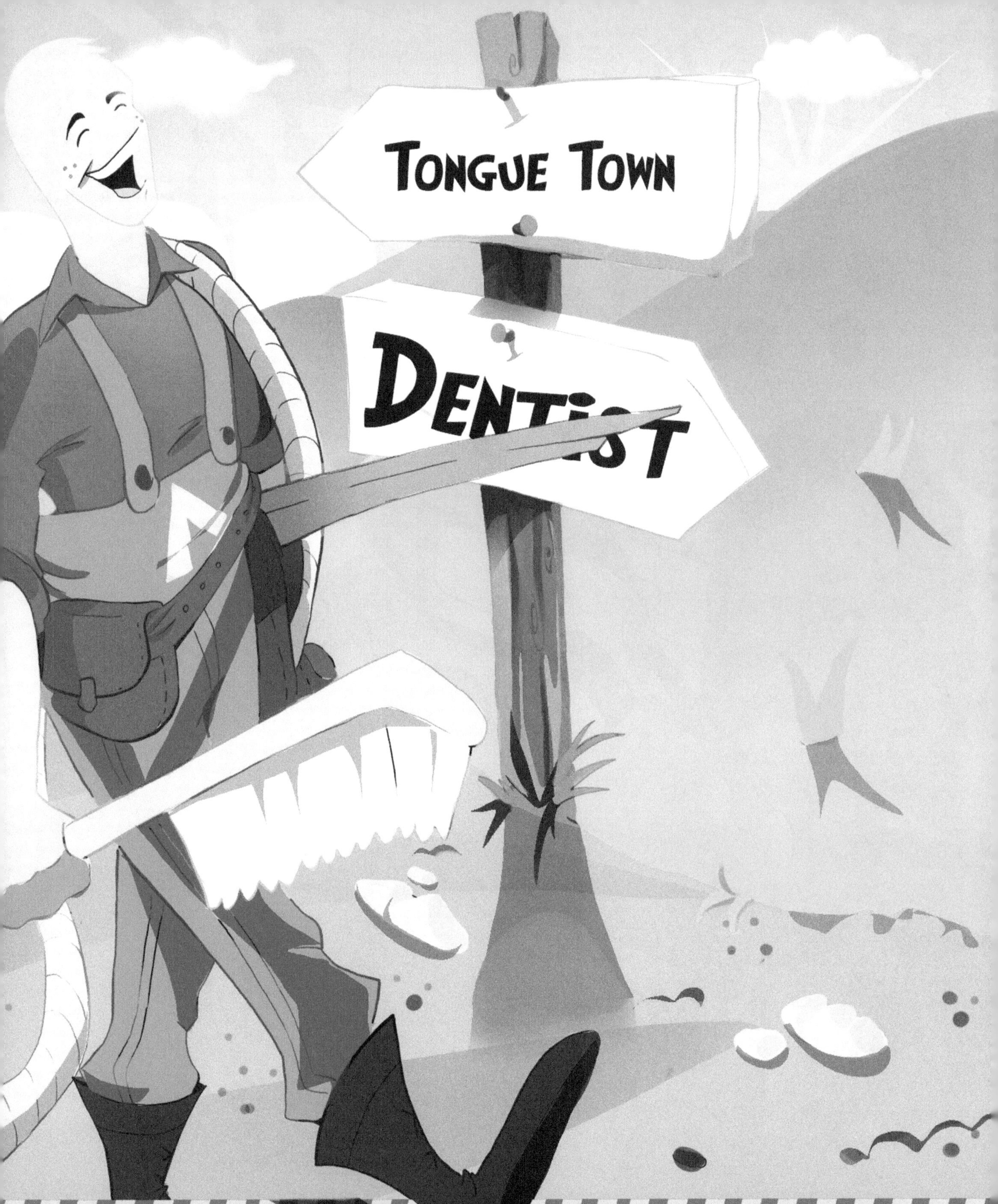
TONGUE TOWN
DENTIST

"Make sure to brush and floss three times a day, folks," the Toothpaste Avenger told them on his way out of town. "That will surely keep those foul creatures away from your beautiful Molar Mountains. Using a toothpick helps too. And watch out for those Candy Critters. I hear they are setting up shop everywhere these days. You sure don't want an invasion from them!"

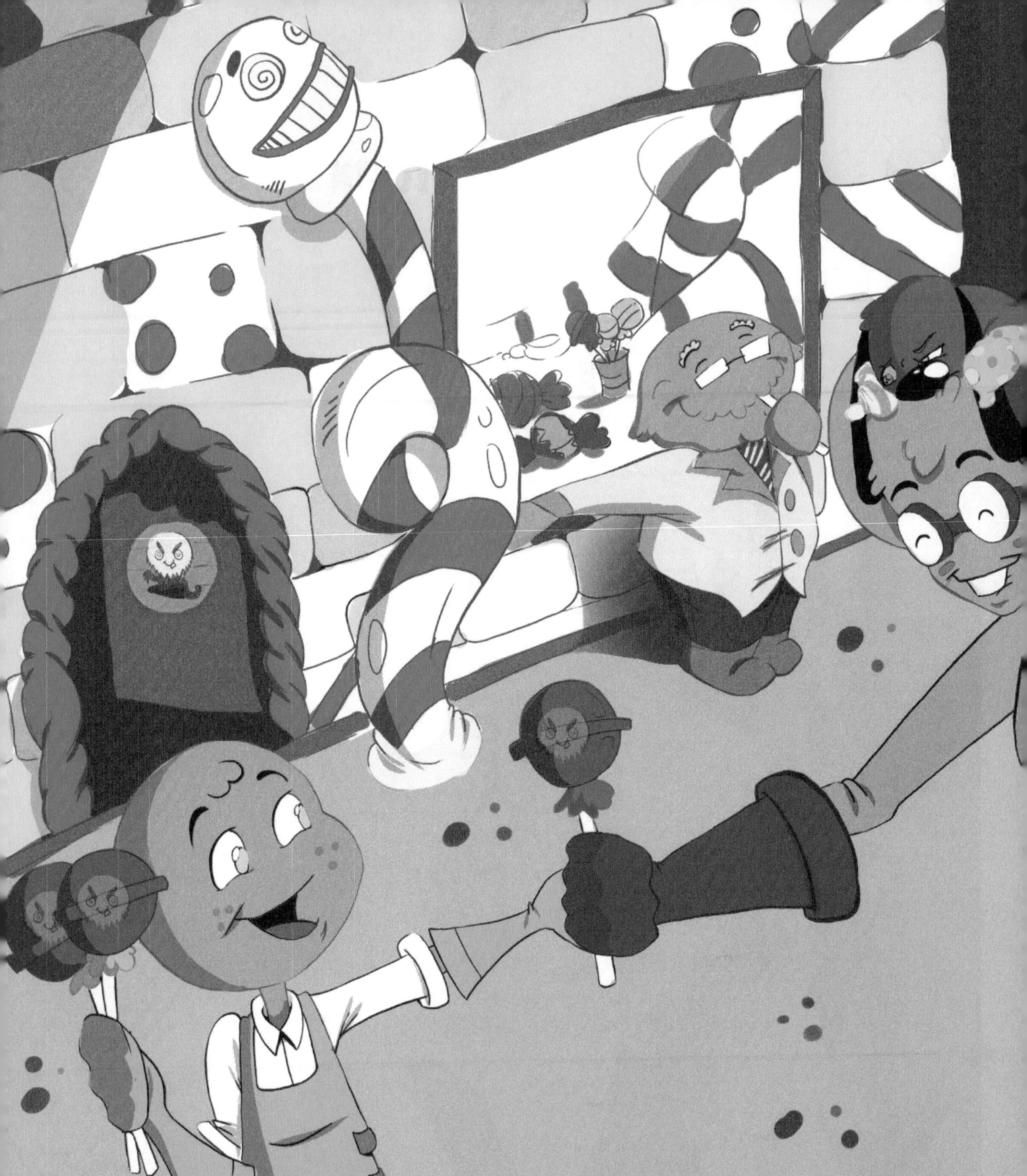

"Candy Critters! Eeek!" yelped Bobby as he gave everyone a celebratory lollipop. "The Cavity Creatures were enough for me. If the Candy Critters are anything like the monsters we just fought, I'm never takin a day off from brushing ever again!"

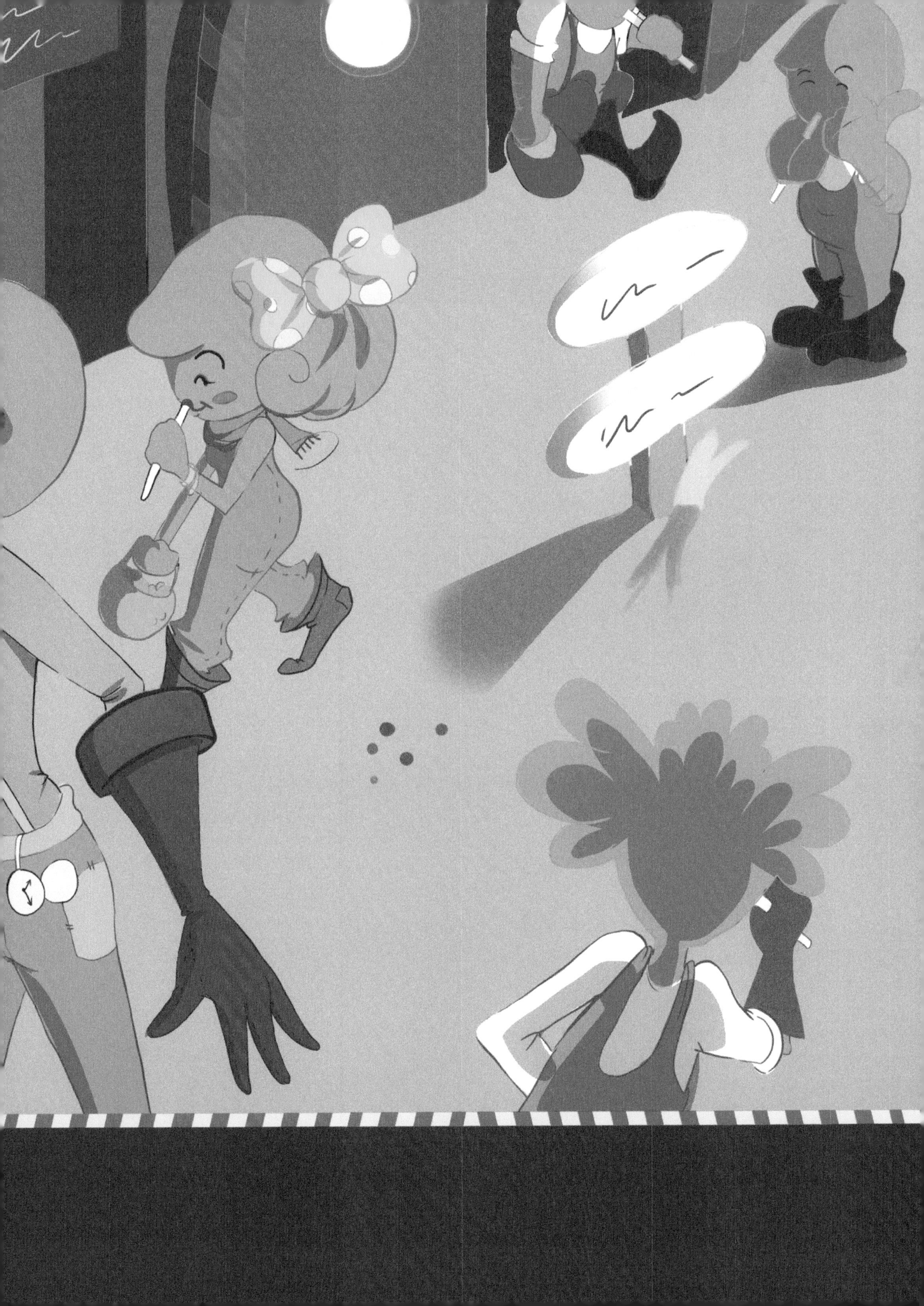

ABOUT THE AUTHOR

Kate Parkhurst lives in Colorado with her husband and two cats. As a primary school teacher, Kate noticed many of her students had one thing in common. They all "claimed" to know how to brush their teeth. Their breath told her otherwise. Inspired to help instill healthy habits in young children's lives, she began a dental checkup program at her school and created the Toothpaste Avenger as a hero for them to look up to.

ABOUT THE ILLUSTRATOR

Eloy Claudio is a fantasy and children's illustrator. *The Invasion of the Cavity Creatures* is his first full-length children's book. Other works include *Doodles Come to Life*, a school program where children's artwork was redrawn professionally. He has put his character design skills to use designing mascots. Born and raised in Brooklyn, NY.,

he makes art with his cat, Umbreon.

CPSIA information can be obtained at www.ICGtesting.com
Printed in the USA
BVOW100531090713

325080BV00001B/1/P